D0770711

The Last Day
of a Condemned Man

Victor Hugo

From *the* 4th French Edition *of* 1832

Watchmaker Publishing

1894

ISBN 978-1-60386-386-5

THE

LAST DAY OF A CONDEMNED.

———◆———

I.

CONDEMNED to death!

For five weeks I have been living with this
thought, always alone with it, always frozen by its
presence, always bending beneath its weight.

Formerly (for it seems to me as if they were years
that had passed, rather than weeks) I was a man
like other men. Every day, every hour, every minute had its own train of thought. My fertile young
imagination was teeming with visions. It amused itself by spreading them out before me one by one, without order and without end, beautifying the coarse,
thin stuff of which life is made with abundance of
embroidery. There were fair maidens and gorgeous
bishop's copes, battles won, theatres full of light and
life, and then more fair maidens and dark avenues at
night under spreading chestnut boughs. In my imagination there were none but holidays. I could
think of what I chose: I was free.

Now I am a prisoner. My body is ironed in
a dungeon, my mind is imprisoned in an idea, — a

horrible, relentless, deathly idea! I have but one thought, one conviction, one certainty: condemned to death!

Whatever I do, the hellish thought is always at my side like a leaden spectre, alone and jealous of intrusion, driving away all hope of distraction, staring wretched, unhappy me in the face, and shaking me with its icy hands when I seek to turn away my head or close my eyes. It glides beneath all the disguises which my mind assumes in order to escape it, mingles like a ghastly refrain with every word which is addressed to me, clings close to my side as I press against the hideous bars of my dungeon, besets my waking hours, haunts my restless slumber, and appears in my dreams in the guise of a knife.

I awake with a start, hunted by it, and saying to myself, "Ah! it is only a dream!" But even before my heavy eyes have had time to open wide enough to see the fatal thought written in the frightful reality which surrounds me, on the damp, sweating flags of my cell, in the flickering rays of my night-light, in the coarse woof of the stuff of which my clothes are made, and on the dark silhouette of the sentry whose musket-barrel glistens through the bars, it seems as if a voice were already whispering in my ear, "Condemned to death!"

II.

It was a beautiful morning in August.

Three days my trial had been in progress; three days my name and my crime had attracted a swarm of spectators, who swooped down upon the benches of the court-room like crows upon a dead body; three days all the phantasmagoria of judges, witnesses, lawyers, king's attorneys, had passed back and forth before my eyes, sometimes grotesque, sometimes truculent, but always ominous and murderous. The first two nights — nights of anxiety and terror — I was unable to sleep; the third night I slept from sheer *ennui* and fatigue. At midnight I left the jurors deliberating. I was taken back to the pallet in my dungeon, and fell at once into a deep sleep, the sleep of utter oblivion. They were the first reposeful hours I had known for many days.

I was still in the very deepest of this deep sleep, when they came to awaken me. This time the heavy tramp of the turnkey's hob-nailed shoes, the jangling of his bunch of keys, and the hoarse groaning of the bolts were not enough: to arouse me from my lethargy needed nothing less than his harsh voice in my ear, and his rough grasp upon my arm : —

"Come, get up !"

I opened my eyes and sat up in terror. At that moment I saw, through the high, narrow window of my cell on the ceiling of the corridor outside, — the only sky which it is my privilege to look upon, — the yellowish reflection, which eyes wonted to the darkness of a prison are so quick to recognize as sunshine. I love the sun.

"It 's a fine morning," I said to the turnkey.

For a moment he made no reply, as if he could not determine whether the question was worth the expenditure of a word; then he muttered surlily, with some effort : —

"Possibly."

I did not move, but, with mind half asleep, and smiling lips, kept my eyes fixed on the soft, golden reflection, which made bright streaks on the ceiling.

"It 's a beautiful day," I repeated.

"Yes," he replied; "they are waiting for you."

These few words, like the thread which arrests the flight of the insect, brought me abruptly back to reality. Again I saw, as in a lightning-flash, the gloomy court-room, the horse-shoe-shaped bench of the judges, laden with blood-stained rags, the three rows of stupid-faced witnesses, the two gendarmes at either end of the bench on which I sat, the black robes moving hither and thither, the heads of the crowd swarming in the shadow at the rear, and, fastened upon my face, the steady gaze of the twelve jurors, who had been awake while I was sleeping !

I rose ; my teeth were chattering, my hands trembled so that I could hardly find my clothes, my legs shook. At the first step I took I stumbled like a street-porter with too heavy a load. However, I followed the jailer.

The two gendarmes were waiting for me at the cell-door. They put handcuffs upon me; they had a complicated little lock which they secured with great care. I made no resistance; it was simply putting one machine upon another.

We passed through an interior courtyard. The crisp morning air revived me. I raised my head. The sky was blue, and the sun's warm rays, intercepted by high chimneys, traced broad shafts and sharp angles of light at the top of the high, frowning walls of the prison. It was, in truth, a lovely day.

We mounted a spiral staircase; we passed through a corridor, then another, then a third, and came to a low door which opened before us. A blast of hot air, bringing with it a vague noise, struck me in the face; it was the breath of the crowd in the court-room. I entered.

At my appearance there was a confused noise of weapons and voices. The people rose noisily from their benches, the partitions cracked; and while I passed down the long room, between two masses of men and women held back by soldiers, I felt that I was the centre from which radiated the wires that moved all those gaping, staring faces.

At that instant I noticed that I was without irons ; but I could not remember where or when they were taken off.

Profound silence followed my entrance. I reached my place. The tumult in my brain ceased simultaneously with the tumult in the crowd. I realized

23

with the suddenness of lightning, what I had hitherto
but vaguely dreamed, that the decisive moment had
come, and I was there to hear my sentence.

Let him who can explain the fact that the manner
in which this perception came to me prevented it
from terrifying me. The windows were open; the
air and the busy hum of the town came freely in;
the room was as bright as for a marriage-feast; the
jubilant rays of the sun marked out the shape of
the windows in bright light upon the floor, or upon
the tables, or against the angle of the walls, and
each ray cut through a great prism of gold dust in
the air.

The judges were sitting in their places with a
satisfied air; probably they were glad to have done
with the affair in good season. The face of the
president, as the soft light from one of the windows
was reflected upon it, had a calm, kindly expression;
and a young associate was talking almost gayly, as
he toyed with his neck-band, with a fair dame in a
red hat, who was favored with a seat behind him.

The jurors alone seemed pale and depressed, but
it was apparently from fatigue, because they had been
awake all night. Some of them were yawning.
There was nothing in their countenances to indicate
that they were about to pronounce sentence of
death; and I could detect no sentiment in the expression of the worthy citizens beyond a longing
desire for sleep.

Directly in front of me was a window wide open.
I could hear the flower-girls laughing on the quay;
and on the window-sill a pretty little yellow plant,

with the sun shining full upon it, was playing with the breeze in a cleft of the stone.

How could any sinister thought force its way in among so many pleasant surroundings? Bathed thus in the fresh air and the sunlight, it was impossible for me to think of anything but freedom ; hope shone as brightly in my heart as the sunshine around me ; and with full confidence in the result, I awaited the verdict as one awaits deliverance and life.

Meanwhile my counsel arrived. They were waiting for him. He had just breakfasted heartily and with good appetite. When he reached his place he leaned over to me with a smile

"I am very hopeful," he said.

"It looks hopeful, does n't it?" I replied, lightly, and smiling back at him.

"Yes," he replied ; "I know nothing yet of their verdict, but they undoubtedly have found that there was no premeditation, and in that case it will be only penal servitude for life."

"What's that, monsieur?" I rejoined indignantly ; "better death a hundred times!"

Yes, death! "And then," some voice within me whispered, "what do I risk by saying that? Was sentence of death ever pronounced except at midnight, by the light of torches, in a dark, gloomy hall, and on a cold, stormy winter's night? Why, in the month of August, at eight o'clock of such a lovely morning and with such kind-hearted jurors, it's impossible!" And my eyes wandered back to the pretty yellow flower in the sun.

Suddenly the president, who had waited only for

my counsel, ordered me to rise. The gendarmes carried arms; as if by an electric shock the whole assemblage was on its feet at the same instant. An insignificant cipher — the clerk, I think — who sat at a table below the bench, began to speak, and read the verdict which the jurors had rendered in my absence. A cold sweat broke out all over my body; I leaned against the wall that I might not fall.

"Mr. Advocate, have you anything to say before sentence is pronounced?" the president asked.

I would have had everything under heaven to say, but not a word came to me. My tongue was glued to my palate.

My defender arose.

I understood that he was seeking to weaken the force of the jury's verdict and to secure the infliction, instead of the penalty which it called for, of that other penalty which it had wounded me so deeply to have him mention as a thing to be hoped for.

My indignation must have been strong to make itself felt among the thousand and one emotions which were disputing possession of my thoughts. I tried to repeat aloud what I had already said to him: "Better death a hundred times!" But the words would not come, and I could only seize him roughly by the arm, crying with convulsive strength: "No!"

The crown-attorney argued against my advocate's contention, and I listened to him with stupid satisfaction. Then the judges went out, and returned in a few moments, when the president read my sentence.

" Condemned to death ! " said the crowd ; and while I was being led away, the whole concourse of people followed on my heels with the uproar of a falling building. I walked on, drunk and stupefied. A revolution had taken place in me. Until the sentence was pronounced, I had felt that my heart beat, and that I breathed and lived in the same atmosphere as other men ; but now I could clearly distinguish something like a barrier between the world and myself Nothing appeared to me in the same light as before. The large windows, flooded with light, the lovely sunshine, the pure sky, the pretty flower, all seemed white and ghostly, of the color of a shroud. The men and women and children who were crowding about me seemed to me like phantoms.

At the foot of the staircase a dirty black vehicle with barred window was awaiting me. As I was entering it, I cast a glance over the square.

" A condemned man ! " cried the passers-by, rushing toward the carriage.

Through the cloud which seemed to have been interposed between myself and the rest of the world, I distinguished two young girls, who were following my movements with eager eyes.

" Good ! " said the younger, clapping her hands, " it will be in six weeks ! "

III.

CONDEMNED to death!

Oh, well! why not? "Men," so I remember to have read in some book, in which this was the only good thing, "men are all condemned to death, with indefinite reprieves." What great change had taken place then in my situation?

Since the hour that my doom was pronounced, how many have died who had counted upon long life! How many have gone before me, who then, young and free and in good health, made their plans to go on a certain day and see my head fall on the Place de Grève! How many who are now walking with heads erect and breathing the free air of heaven, going in and out at will, will perhaps go before me ere that day comes!

And after all, what is there about this life that I should regret? Indeed, the depressing obscurity and the black bread of my dungeon, the ration of thin soup taken from the galley-slaves' trough, the being cursed at and treated like a brute by turnkeys and keepers, — I, who have the refinement that goes with education, — the being deprived of intercourse with a single human being who thinks me worthy a civil word, and to whom I can return it, and the incessant, shuddering fear both of what I have done, and of what they will do to me, — such are almost the only blessings of which the executioner can deprive me.

Ah! no matter; it is fearful!

IV.

THE black vehicle transported me to this place, this hideous Bicêtre.

Seen from afar, there is something majestic in the aspect of this edifice; it unfolds itself to the view on the brow of a hill, and at a distance retains some traces of its old-time splendor, — the air of a royal château. But as you draw near, the palace becomes a hovel. The dilapidated gables offend the eye. I cannot describe the shameful, impoverished appearance of these royal façades: one would say that the walls had the leprosy. There is no glass in the windows, but heavy iron bars, up and down and across, and here and there the haggard face of a galley-slave or a madman glued to them.

Such is life, seen at close quarters.

V.

I HAD scarcely arrived when iron hands took possession of me. They multipled their precautions; no knife, no fork for my meals; the strait-jacket, a sort of canvas sack, imprisoned my arms. They were responsible for my life. I had filed an appeal; the decision of so weighty an affair might be delayed for six or seven weeks, and it was important to keep me safe and sound for the Place de Grève.

The first days I was treated with a gentleness which was horrible to me. The kind consideration of a turnkey has a flavor of the scaffold. Fortunately, after a few days, long habit recovered the upper hand; they confused me with the other prisoners, and treated us all with equal brutality, and there was no more of that anomalous courteous distinction which kept the executioner forever in my mind. That was not the only change for the better. My youth, my docility, the assiduity of the prison-chaplain, and, more than all else, a few words in Latin which I addressed to the concierge, who failed to understand them, procured me the privilege of a walk once a week with the other prisoners, and effected the disappearance of the strait-jacket, which paralyzed me. After much hesitation they also gave me pen, ink, paper, and a lamp at night.

Every Sunday after mass, I am allowed to walk in the yard at the recreation hour. There, I talk

with the prisoners; I have no choice but to do it.
They are well-meaning fellows, poor wretches. They
tell me of their exploits; it would make me shudder
with horror to hear them, except that I know they
are boasting. They teach me to talk *argot*, —
"*rouscailler bigorne*," as they say. It is a dialect
engrafted upon our ordinary language, a revolting.
excrescence, a wart. Sometimes it is singularly en-
ergetic, and there is something picturesquely horrible
about it; for instance: *Il y a du raisiné sur le
trimar*, "There's blood upon the road;" *épouser la
veuve*,[1] "to be hanged," — as if the gallows-rope
were the widow of all those who are hanged by it.
A thief's head has two names, — the *sorbonne*, when
he is planning or advising crime, and the *tronche*,
when the executioner cuts it off. Sometimes there
is a touch of the vaudeville: a *cachemire d'osier*
means a ragman's basket, and *la menteuse*,[2] the
tongue. And then they are continually letting drop
strange, mysterious, ugly words, whose origin no
one can say; in their mouths the executioner is
le taule, death *la cône*, and the place of execution
la placarde. One would say that they were toads
and spiders. When one hears this jargon it is as if
some one were shaking a lot of dusty, filthy rags
before one.

However, these men pity me, and they are the
only ones who do. The jailers, keepers, and turnkeys — I bear them no ill-will for it — talk and
laugh, and speak of me to my face as if I were an
inanimate thing.

[1] Literally — to marry the widow.   [2] Literally — the liar.

VI.

I SAID to myself: As I have writing materials
why should I not write? But what to write? Confined between four walls of bare, cold stone, with no
power to go abroad, with nothing to look at, and
with nothing under heaven to distract my thoughts,
except to follow on the dark wall the slow movement of the square of sickly light which comes in
through the peep-hole in the door, and, as I said just
now, alone with one thought, a thought of crime
and punishment, of murder and death, — how can I
have aught to say, who have nothing more to do on
earth? What can I hope to find in this withered,
empty brain, worth the trouble of being written?

But why not? If all my surroundings are monotonous and colorless, is there not a tempest, a bitter
struggle, a grim tragedy raging within me?

Does not this fixed idea which haunts me present
itself to me every hour, every instant, in a new guise,
always more ghastly and more relentless in propor-
tion as the end draws nigh? Why should I not try
to describe to myself all the violent and unfamiliar
emotions which I feel in my abandoned, hopeless
condition? Surely, the matter is abundant; and
though my days are few, there will be enough of
anguish and terror and torture crowded into them to
wear out this pen, and exhaust the inkstand. More-

over the only way to diminish my suffering from my anguish of mind is to examine it closely, and the attempt to describe it may divert me.

It may be, too, that what I write will not be altogether useless. Will not this journal of my suffering, hour by hour, minute by minute, pang by pang, if I have the strength to carry it on until the moment when it is *physically* impossible for me to go further with it, this narrative of my sensations, necessarily unfinished, but as complete as possible, — will it not, I say, convey a weighty and valuable lesson? Will there not be in this record of the agonizing thought, in this constant progression of suffering, in this sort of intellectual autopsy of a condemned man, more than one lesson for those who condemn him? Perhaps the perusal of these pages may make their hand somewhat less hasty, when they are inclined hereafter to toss a head which encloses a brain, a man's head, into what they call the scales of justice. Perhaps they, poor wretches, have never reflected on the slow succession of tortures comprised in the glib formula of a death-sentence. Have they ever thought of this one point, for instance, — that this man, whom they are putting away, has an intellectual faculty which counted upon life, and a soul which is not prepared to die? No. They see in it all nothing but the fall of a triangular knife, and think, beyond a doubt, that, so far as the condemned man is concerned, there is nothing before, nothing after.

These pages will undeceive them. If some day they are published they will direct their minds to the thought of the mind's suffering; for that is what they have no suspicion of. They are very exultant in their power to kill with almost no physical suffering. Ah! that is a matter of the slightest consequence! What is physical suffering, in comparison with mental suffering? Horror and pity, to think that laws are made thus! A day will come, and perhaps these jottings, the last confidant of a wretched mortal, will contribute, — unless after my death these bits of paper are thrown into the mud of the yard for the wind to play with, or are glued to a turnkey's broken window-pane, there to rot in the rain.

VII.

THAT what I write here may some day be of use
to others, that it may furnish food for thought to the
judge when he is about to render judgment, that it
may save some poor unfortunate, innocent or guilty,
from the agony which I am doomed to suffer, — what
is all this to me? What matters it? When my head
has fallen, what harm will it do me that other heads
fall? Can it be that I really had such an absurd
thought? — to throw down the scaffold after I have
suffered on it! I pray to know what advantage will
come to me from that?

What! the sunshine, the lovely springtime, the
blooming fields, the birds that sing in the morning,
the clouds, the trees, nature, liberty, life, — all these
have no more existence for me?

Ah! I am the one to be saved! Is it true, is 'it
really true, that that cannot be, that I must die to-
morrow, perhaps to-day, and that there is no escape?
Oh, God! The horrible thought has come to me to
dash out my brains against my dungeon wall!

VIII.

LET us reckon how long I have to live.

Three days' delay after the decree allowing the appeal.

A week of forgetfulness in the prosecutor's office of the assize-court, after which the documents are sent to the minister.

A fortnight's waiting at the office of the minister, who does not so much as know that they exist, but who is supposed, nevertheless, to transmit them, after examination, to the Court of Appeal.

There, classification, numbering, and recording; for the guillotine is overworked, and every one has to wait his turn.

Another fortnight, to make sure that no injustice is done you.

At last the court assembles, generally on a Thursday, dismisses twenty appeals in a mass, and sends all the cases back to the minister, who sends them to the prosecutor, who sends them to the executioner. Three days.

On the morning of the fourth day the deputy crown-attorney says to himself as he adjusts his cravat, "We must wind up this matter." Thereupon if the deputy-clerk has no breakfast-party to prevent him from attending to his duties, the order for the execution is entered, drawn up, copied in a fair hand, and despatched ; and at dawn the next morning the sound of hammers is heard on the Place de Grève, and the hoarse-voiced criers are shouting at the street-corners.

Six weeks in all.   The girl was right.

Now, here I have been at least five weeks, perhaps six (I dare not count them up), in this gloomy Bicêtre, and I believe that three days hence will be Thursday.

IX.

I HAVE made my will?

For what purpose? I am sentenced to pay the costs, and the little I have will hardly suffice for that. The guillotine is a very expensive amusement.

I leave a mother, I leave a wife, I leave a child.

A little girl of three, a sweet, red-cheeked darling, with great black eyes, and long chestnut curls.

She was a month more than two years old when I last saw her.

Thus, when I am dead, there will be these three, childless, husbandless, fatherless; three orphans of different varieties; three widows by the act of the law.

I admit that I am justly punished; but what have those innocent creatures done? That makes no difference; they are dishonored, they are ruined. Such is justice!

It is not that the thought of my poor old mother distresses me; she is sixty-four years old, and the blow will kill her. Or if she does live on a few days, she will say nothing, provided she has a few hot ashes in her warming-pan to the last.

Nor am I worried about my wife; she is in feeble health already, her mind is weak, and she will die too.

That is to say, unless she goes mad ; they say that that conduces to long life, but at all events her mind does not suffer; it sleeps, it is dead to all intent.

But my daughter, my baby, my poor little Marie, who is laughing and playing and singing at this moment, without a care, — it is the thought of her that tears my heart!

X.

A WORD of description of my dungeon.

Eight feet square ; four walls of hewn stone rising from a flagged floor, a step higher than the gallery outside.

At the right of the door, as one enters, a sort of recess, a burlesque of an alcove. A bunch of straw is tossed down there, on which the prisoner is supposed to rest and sleep, dressed in cotton drawers and a drill waistcoat, winter and summer.

Above my head, by way of sky, is a black arch, *ogive*-shaped, — so it is called, — from which thick spider's-webs hang like rags.

For the rest, no windows, not even an air-hole ; a door of wood cased in iron.

I am wrong ; in the centre of the door, toward the top, is an opening nine inches square, with crossed iron bars ; the turnkey can close it at night.

Without is a corridor of considerable length, lighted and ventilated by means of narrow air-holes at the top of the wall, and divided into compart-ments by partitions of solid masonry, which com-municate with one another by a series of low, arched doors. Each of these compartments serves as a sort of anteroom for a cell similar to mine. In these cells the convicts are confined when they are subjected to punishment. The first three are reserved for those under sentence of death, because they are the nearest to the main prison, and hence most convenient for the jailer.

These cells are all that remains of the old castle of Bicêtre, as it was built in the fifteenth century, by the Cardinal of Winchester, by whom Jeanne d'Arc was burned at the stake. I heard a keeper give this information to the curiosity-seekers who came to see me the other day in my cell, and stared at me from a distance as if I were a wild beast in a menagerie. The keeper had a hundred sous from them.

I forgot to say that there is a sentry on guard at the door of my cell, night and day, and I never lift my eyes to the square hole that I do not see his eyes, always wide open and fixed upon me.

By the way, there is supposed to be light and air in this stone box of mine.

XI.

As daylight has not yet arrived, how shall I employ the darkness? I have an idea. I have left my bed, and am examining the four walls of my cell by the light of my lamp. They are covered with writing, with drawings, and strange figures, and names which overlap and efface one another. It seems as if every condemned man that ever occupied it was determined to leave his mark, here at least, if nowhere else. There are pencil marks and chalk and charcoal, black letters, white letters, gray letters, many cut deep in the rock, and here and there rusty-looking characters which one would swear were traced with blood. Surely, if my mind were more at liberty, I should be deeply interested in this strange book, page after page of which meets my eyes on every stone in this cell. I should like to put together all these fragments of thought, scattered over the flags; conjure up a man for each name; restore sense and life to these mutilated inscriptions, disjointed phrases, maimed words, — headless bodies now, like those who wrote them.

By my bed are two bleeding hearts, pierced by an arrow, and above them is written, "Love for life." The poor devil did not bind himself for long.

Near by is something like a three-cornered hat, with a small figure roughly sketched above, and these words: " Vive l'empereur ! 1824."

More bleeding hearts with this inscription, well suited to a prison: " I love and adore Mathieu Danvin. JACQUES."

On the opposite wall is the one word: "PAPA-VOINE." The capital P. is elaborately ornamented with arabesques.

I notice a verse from an immoral song.

There is also a liberty cap, cut deep in the rock, with this beneath it: " BORIES — La République." He was one of the four non-commissioned officers at La Rochelle. Poor boy ! What ghastly things these alleged political necessities are ! For an idea, a dream, a mere abstraction, the penalty is this frightful thing they call the guillotine ! — while I complain, I, a miserable wretch, who have committed a real crime, who have shed another's blood !

I will go no farther in my examination. I just saw, done in white chalk at the corner of the wall, a revolting sketch, a sketch of the scaffold, which is being erected for me, it may be, at this very hour. My lamp was near falling from my hands.

XII.

I RETURNED hastily to my bundle of straw, and sat down upon it, with my head between my knees. Then my childish terror passed away, and I felt an intense curiosity to continue to read my wall.

Beside the name of Papavoine was a huge spider's-web, thickened with dust, and stretched across the corner of the wall. I swept it away and beneath it were four or five names perfectly legible, among many others of which nothing remained but a mark or two : —

"DAUTUN, 1815; POULAIN, 1818; JEAN MARTIN, 1821; CASTAING, 1823."

I read these names, and they awoke distressing memories. Dautun was the man who cut his brother into four pieces, went into Paris at night, and threw the head into a fountain, and the body into a drain. Poulain murdered his wife. Jean Martin fired a pistol at his father as he was in the act of opening a window. Castaing was the physician who poisoned his friend, then attended him in the illness he had himself caused, and administered the poison a second time, instead of an antidote. And Papavoine! the fiendish madman who killed his children by stabbing them about the head!

And these, I said to myself, as a feverish shudder shook my limbs, these are the men who have occupied this cell before me! Here on these same flags whereon I am standing now, they thought their last thoughts, — these men of murder and of blood! in this contracted space, along these walls, they took their last steps on earth like caged wild beasts. They succeeded one another after brief intervals; it seems that this dungeon is never empty. They left the place warm, — left it warm for me. And I, when my turn comes, shall join them in the cemetery at Clamart, where the grass grows so fast.

I am neither a dreamer nor superstitious, and it is probable that these thoughts induced an attack of fever; for while they were running through my brain, it suddenly seemed to me as if those fatal names were written in fire on the black wall; there came a ringing in my ears, which grew more and more pronounced, and there was a red glare over everything. Then it seemed as if the cell was full of men, strange men who carried their heads in their left hands, and carried them by the mouths because they had no hair. All shook their fists at me, except the parricide.

I closed my eyes in horror, but saw it all then more distinctly than before.

Whether it was a dream, a phantom or a reality, I should have gone mad, if a sudden shock had not aroused me just in time. I was almost falling when I felt a cold body with hairy legs crawling on my bare foot; it was the spider that I had driven from its home.

That restored my self-control, — Oh, those fearful

spectres ! — No, it was a mist, a creation of my throbbing brain.   A phantom *à la* Macbeth !   The dead are dead, especially those fellows.   They are securely locked into the tomb.   That is a prison from which the prisoners do not escape.   How happened it, then, that I was so afraid ?

The door of the tomb cannot be opened from within.

XIII.

I HAVE seen a hideous thing these last few days.

It was broad daylight, and the prison was full of bustle. I could hear the heavy doors open and close, the iron bolts and padlocks grinding, and the bunches of keys jingling at the jailers' belts; the stairways shook from top to bottom under the steps that went hurrying up and down, and voices were calling back and forth from end to end of the long corridors. My immediate neighbors, the convicts under punishment, seemed more light-hearted than usual. All Bicêtre seemed to be laughing and singing and dancing and frisking about.

I, the only one dumb in all the hubbub, the only one motionless in the commotion, listened in wondering expectation.

A jailer passed my door.

I ventured to call to him and ask if it was a holiday in the prison.

"Holiday, if you choose to call it so," he replied. "They are going to iron the convicts who are to start for Toulon to-morrow. Would you like to see it done? It will amuse you."

It is a fact that any spectacle, however revolting, is a God-send to a solitary recluse. I accepted the opportunity to be amused.

The keeper took the customary precautions to make sure of me, then led me into a small, empty cell, absolutely without furniture, which had a grated window, — a real window breast-high, through which the sky could really be seen.

"There," he said, "you can see and hear from this window. You will be alone in your box like the king."

He went out and locked and padlocked and bolted me in.

The window looked out upon a square courtyard of considerable size; on each of the four sides a tall, six-story building of hewn stone arose like a wall. Nothing can be conceived more dilapidated, more naked, and more depressing to the sight than this quadruple façade, pierced by many grated windows, to which, from top to bottom, were glued innumerable thin and pallid faces, crowded one above another like the stones of a wall, and all framed, so to speak, by the squares formed by the intersecting bars. They were the prisoners, spectators of the ceremony, pending the arrival of the day when they should be actors therein. One might have taken them for souls in torment looking out into hell through the air-holes of purgatory.

They were all gazing in silence at the still empty courtyard. They were waiting. Among those dull and hopeless faces, a pair of bright, piercing eyes shone out here and there like coals of fire.

The buildings which surround the courtyard do not shut it out altogether from the outside world. One of the four sides (the one toward the east) is divided near its centre, and the two portions are connected by an iron grating. This grating gives entrance to a second yard, smaller than the first, and like it surrounded by walls and blackened gable-ends.

All around the main courtyard are stone benches against the walls. In the centre is an upright iron rod, curved at the top, intended to hold a lantern.

The noon hour struck. A wide gate, hidden in a recess of the wall, was suddenly thrown open. A wagon, escorted by disgracefully filthy soldiers, in blue uniforms with red epaulets and yellow cross-belts, rumbled into the courtyard with a sound of clanking iron. It was the convict tumbril and the fetters.

On the instant, as if that noise awoke all the latent noise in the prison, the spectators at the windows, who had hitherto been silent and motionless, broke forth in shouts of joy, songs, threats, and imprecations, mingled with bursts of laughter most painful to hear. It was as if one were looking on at a masquerade of demons. On every face was a fiendish grimace, fists were thrust out between the bars, every voice was howling, every eye was flashing, and I was terrified to see such a shower of sparks rise from those ashes.

Meanwhile the keepers, among whom I could distinguish, by their civilian's clothes and their fright, some curiosity-seekers from Paris, set calmly about their work. One of them mounted the cart, and threw down to his comrades the chains, the neck-irons, and the bundles of cotton-trousers. Thereupon they divided up the work; some took the long chains,

which are called *ficelles* in the prison *argot*, and laid
them out along the ground in one courtyard ; others
unfolded the *taffetas*, that is to say, shirts and trousers, upon the pavement, while the more experienced,
under the eye of their leader, a short, thickset old
man, examined the iron necklets one by one, and
then tested them by striking them against the flags.
All this amid the satirical shouts of the prisoners,
which rose above all the other noises except the up-
roarious laughter of the convicts for whom the prep-
arations were being made, and who were relegated
to the windows of the old prison looking upon the
smaller courtyard.

When the preliminaries were at an end, a gentleman in a gold-embroidered uniform, who was addressed as *Monsieur l'inspecteur*, gave an order to the
warden of the prison ; and lo, a moment later, two
or three low doors vomited out into the courtyard,
almost at the same instant, and as if they were blown
in by puffs of wind, a swarm of ghastly, howling,
ragged men. They were the convicts.

When they appeared, the delight of the occupants
of the windows redoubled. Some of the convicts,
the celebrated names of the galleys, were greeted
with acclamations and applause, which they received
with a sort of proud modesty. Most of them wore
hats woven with their own hands from the straw
given them to sleep on, all of strange shape, so that
the hat might attract attention to the head within it
in the towns through which they passed. These last
were even more warmly applauded. One in partic-
ular aroused a frenzy of enthusiasm, — a youth of

seventeen with a girl's face. He came from the
dungeons where he had been confined in secret for a
week; he had made from his bunch of straw a gar-
ment which enveloped him from head to foot, and he
came into the courtyard turning handsprings with
the agility of a snake. He was a clown sentenced
for theft. There was a perfect tornado of hand-clap-
ping and yells of delight. The galley-slaves answered
it; and a truly frightful thing it was, this interchange
of courtesies between the titular galley-slaves and
those who aspired to that distinction. In vain was
society represented there by the jailers, and the terrified sensation seekers, — crime defied them to their
faces, and made of this horrible punishment a sort
of family holiday.

As fast as they arrived they were driven between
two lines of keepers into the smaller courtyard, where
they were to be examined by the physician. There
they all made a last effort to escape the journey, alleg-
ing some excuse based upon their physical condition,
— weak eyes, lame legs, or mutilated hands. But
almost all were found to be sound enough for the
galleys, and they resigned themselves to the prospect
with a great show of indifference, forgetting in a few
moments the infirmities of a whole lifetime.

The grating leading into the small yard was opened
again. A keeper called the roll in alphabetical order,
and each convict, as his name was called, came out
into the large courtyard again, and took his stand
in a corner beside some companion whose initial let-
ter chanced to be the same. Thus every one found
himself thrown upon his own resources, every one

had to carry his own chain beside a stranger; and if by any chance a convict had a friend, the chain separated them. The last of misfortunes.

When about thirty had come out the grating was closed. A keeper lined them up with his stick, throwing to each man a shirt, a waistcoat, and a pair of coarse linen trowsers; then he made a sign and they all began to undress. An unforeseen incident happened just in time to change their humiliation to torture.

Up to this time the weather had been fine, and although the October air was somewhat chilly, from time to time there was a rift in the gray clouds, and a ray of sunshine broke through. But the convicts had just thrown off their prison rags, and were standing there stark naked to undergo the careful scrutiny of the keepers, and the inquisitive gaze of the strangers who walked around them to look at their shoulders, when the sky grew dark, a cold autumn shower came up without warning, and the rain poured down in sheets on the uncovered heads and bare bodies of the galley-slaves, and their wretched clothing which lay spread out on the ground.

In a twinkling the yard was cleared of all except keepers and convicts. The idlers from Paris sought shelter in the doorways.

The rain continued to fall in floods. There was now nobody to be seen in the courtyard save the naked convicts, with the water streaming down from them upon the flooded pavement. Gloomy silence had succeeded their noisy bravado. They were shivering, their teeth were chattering, their meagre legs and bony knees rattled against one another; it was pitiful to see them hurrying to cover their bodies, blue with cold, with the soaked shirts and waist-coats and trousers. It would have been better to remain naked.

One only, an old man, retained some animation. He cried out, as he wiped himself with his damp shirt, that "this was not in the programme;" then began to laugh and shook his fist at the sky.

When they had donned their travelling costume, they were taken in bands of twenty or thirty to the other corner of the yard, where the chains were stretched out along the ground awaiting them. They are long and very strong, and have other short chains attached to them two feet apart. At each end of these shorter chains is a square neckiron, which opens on a hinge at one corner, and is fastened at the opposite corner by an iron pin; it is riveted around the galley-slave's neck for the journey. When the chains are spread out on the ground they much resemble the backbone of a fish.

They made the convicts sit down in the mud on the drenched pavement, and tried the necklets on them; then two smiths provided with portable an-vils riveted them on with a heavy iron hammer. It is a fearful moment, when the cheek of the bold-est pales. Each blow of the hammer, dealt upon the anvil which is set close against the prisoner's back, sends his chin into the air; the slightest back-ward movement of the head, and his skull would be crushed like a walnut.

After this operation they became very gloomy.

Nothing could be heard but the clanking of the chains, and now and then a shout, and the dull sound of the keeper's staff upon the legs of the unruly ones. There were some who wept. The old men shivered and bit their lips. I gazed in terror at all the scowling faces in their iron frames.

Thus after the inspection by the physicians came the inspection by the jailers; after the inspection by the jailers, the ironing. A drama in three acts.

Once more a ray of sunshine made its appearance. You would have said that it set fire to all their brains. They rose together, as by a spasmodic movement. The five chains joined hands, and suddenly formed in an immense ring around the lantern-rod. They rushed around until one's eyes were dizzy looking at them. They sang a song of the galleys, a romance in slang, to an air which was at times plaintive, and at times fast and furious; at intervals shrill cries and gasping, heart-rending bursts of laughter, mingled with the mysterious words; wild shouts of applause followed, and the chains clanking in cadence furnished an orchestral accompaniment to the song which was even more hoarse and rasping than the noise they made. If I were seeking a picture of the witches' Sabbath, I would ask for none better or worse than that.

A large trough was brought into the yard. The keepers broke up the convicts' dance with blows of their clubs, and led them up to the trough, which contained a mass of herbs of some sort, swimming in a smoking, greasy liquid. They ate.

Having eaten, they threw what remained of their

25

soup and brown bread upon the ground, and began again to dance and sing. It seems that they are allowed this license on the day they are ironed and the following night.

I watched this strange scene with such intense, eager, breathless interest that I fairly forgot myself. A feeling of profound pity moved me to the very bottom of my soul, and their laughter made me weep.

Suddenly, through the mist of the deep revery in which I was plunged, I saw the howling crowd come to a standstill, and cease their noise. Then every eye was turned upon the window at which I was standing.

"The condemned man! the condemned man!" they cried, pointing at me; and they shouted their delight louder than ever.

I stood as if turned to stone.

I have no idea how they had heard of me, or how they recognized me.

"Good-day! good-evening!" they shrieked with their blood-curdling laughter. One of the youngest, a livid-faced youth, under sentence to the galleys for life, looked enviously at me, as he said: —

"He's in luck! he will be *clipped!* Adieu, comrade!"

I cannot describe my sensations, I was indeed their comrade. The Place de Grève is the sister of Toulon. I was even lower than they; they did me honor. I shuddered.

Yes, their comrade! And a few days later I might have furnished an entertainment for them.

I remained at the window motionless, paralyzed. But when I saw the five chains rushing toward me with expressions of infernal cordiality ; when I heard the discordant clanking of their fetters, and their shouting and tramping at the foot of the wall, it seemed to me as if the swarm of demons were climbing up to my wretched cell ; I cried out, I threw myself against the door with force enough almost to break it, but there was no escape for me ; the bolts were shot on the outside. I beat upon the door, and called for help in a frenzy of terror. I fancied I could hear the awful voices of the convicts approaching. I thought I could see their ghastly faces appearing above my window-sill ; I shrieked again in agony, and fell in a swoon.

XIV.

WHEN I came to myself, it was after nightfall. I was lying upon a cot; by the flickering light of a lantern near the ceiling I saw a row of other cots on either side of my own. I understood that I had been taken to the infirmary.

I lay awake for a few moments, without memory, and with no thought for anything save the happiness of being in bed once more. Certain it is that in other days the thought of that bed in a prison hospital would have filled me with disgust and pity; but I was no longer the same man. The sheets were grayish white and rough to the touch, the blanket thin and full of holes; I could feel the husks through the mattress; but what did that matter? I could stretch my legs at will between the coarse sheets; and under the blanket, thin as it was, I gradually got rid of the horrible chill in the very marrow of my bones to which I had become accustomed.

I fell asleep again. I was awakened by a loud noise just at daybreak. The noise came from outside; my bed was beside the window, and I sat up to see what was going on.

The window looked out on the large courtyard. It was filled with people; two lines of veterans had

great difficulty in keeping a narrow passageway
across the yard free from the crowd. Between
these two lines of soldiers, five long tumbrils loaded
with men jolted slowly along over the pavements.
It was the convicts just setting out.

The vehicles were open. Each chain occupied
one. The convicts were sitting in two rows upon
the sides, back to back, and separated by the common chain, which ran from end to end. I could hear
their irons rattle, and at every jolt I could see their
heads shake, and their hanging legs wave about.

A fine, penetrating rain gave an icy chill to the air,
and glued to their knees their cotton trousers, which
changed from gray to black. The water ran in
streams from their long beards and short hair ; their
faces were purple ; I could see them shiver, and
their teeth were chattering with cold and wrath.
However, they could not move. Once riveted to
the chain a man ceases to be anything more than a
fraction of that hideous whole which is called a *cor-
don*, and which moves like one man. The intellect
must needs abdicate, — the neck-iron of the galleys condemns it to death; and the animal himself
is henceforth forbidden to have needs and appetites
save at certain stated times.

Sitting thus without moving, most of them half-
naked, with bare heads and hanging feet, they began
their journey of twenty-five days, always packed close
upon the same wagons, and clad in the same clothing for the burning sun of July as for the cold rains
of November. One would think that man wished
to share the duties of executioner with the weather.

Some revolting conversation, I know not what, was carried on between the crowd and the wagons; insults on the one hand, bravado on the other, and imprecations on both; but, at a sign from the leader I saw blows rain down at hazard among the living freight, on their heads or their shoulders, and that sort of external tranquillity which is called *order* ensued. But their eyes gleamed with the thirst for revenge, and the poor devils' fists clinched as they lay on their knees.

The five tumbrils, escorted by mounted gendarmes and keepers on foot, disappeared one after another through the high-arched gateway of Bicêtre; they were followed by a sixth, in which cooking utensils, copper dishes, and spare chains were dancing about pell-mell. Some keepers, who had loitered at the canteen, went out on the run to join their squad. The crowd dispersed. The whole scene faded away like a dream. The dull rumbling of the wheels and the clatter of the horses' feet on the paved Fontainebleau road, the cracking of whips, the clanking of chains, and the shouting of the mob wishing ill fortune to the convicts, gradually died away in the distance.

And for them this is but the beginning.

What was it that my advocate said? The galleys! Ah! yes, better death a thousand times, better the scaffold than the galleys; better annihilation than hell; better to offer one's neck to Dr. Guillotin's knife than to the convict's necklet! The galleys! great heaven!

XV.

UNFORTUNATELY I was not ill. The next day I was obliged to leave the infirmary. The dungeon claimed me again.

Not ill! in truth I am young and healthy and strong. The blood flows freely in my veins; all my limbs obey my every whim; I am robust in body and in mind, built to live long; yes, that is all true; and yet I have a disease, a fatal disease, a disease brought on by the hand of man.

Since I left the infirmary, a painful thought has occurred to me, a thought well calculated to drive me mad; it is that I might perhaps have escaped if they had left me there. The doctors and the Sisters of Charity seemed to take great interest in me. To die so young and such a death! One would have said they pitied me, they thronged so around my pillow. Bah! mere curiosity! And then, these people who cure will cure you of a fever, but not of a sentence of death. And yet that would be so easy for them to do! just an open door! What harm could it do them?

No more opportunity now! my appeal will be dismissed, because everything was done in proper form; the witnesses bore true witness, the pleaders pleaded well, the judges gave an impartial judgment. I base no hopes upon it, unless —   But no, madness! there is no hope!   An appeal is a cord which holds you suspended over the abyss, and you can hear it cracking every instant until it breaks.   It is as if the knife of the guillotine took six weeks to fall.

Suppose I were pardoned? Pardoned! By whom, pray? and why? and how?   It is impossible that I should be pardoned.   The example! as they say.

I have but three more steps to take: Bicêtre, the Conciergerie, and the Grève.

XVI.

During the few hours I remained in the infirmary I was sitting by a window, in the sun, — it had reappeared, — or at least in all of it that the bars of the window allowed me to enjoy.

I was sitting there with my head lying heavy in my hands, which found it more than they could carry, my elbows on my knees, and my feet on the rounds of my chair; for my dejection made me bend my back and double myself up as if I had no bones in my limbs, nor muscles in my body.

The stifling odor of the prison affected me more than ever, the chains of the galley-slaves were still rattling in my ears, and I felt deathly weary of Bicêtre. It seemed the good God might well take pity on me, and send me at least a little bird to sing on the edge of the roof opposite me.

I cannot say whether it was the good God or the devil who heard my wish; but almost at the same instant a voice arose under my window, — not the voice of a bird, but, far better, the pure, fresh, velvety voice of a girl of fifteen. I raised my head with a start, and listened intently to the song she was singing. It was a slow, languorous air, a sort of cooing, sad and plaintive. These were the words: —

> C'est dans la rue du Mail
> Où j'ai été coltigé,
> Maluré,

Par trois coquins de railles,
    Lirlonfa malurette,
Sur mes sique' ont foncé,
    Lirlonfa maluré.

Words cannot describe my disappointment.   The
voice went on : —

Sur mes sique' ont foncé,
        Maluré.
Ils m'ont mis la tartouve,
    Lirlonfa malurette,
Grand Meudon est aboulé
    Lirlonfa maluré.
Dans mon trimin rencontre,
    Lirlonfa malurette,
Un peigre du quartier,
    Lirlonfa maluré.

Un peigre du quartier,
        Maluré.
Va t'en dire à ma largue
    Lirlonfa malurette,
Que je suis enfourraillé,
    Lirlonfa maluré.
Ma largue tout en colère,
    Lirlonfa malurette,
M'dit : Qu'as tu donc morfillé ?
    Lirlonfa maluré.

M'dit : Qu'as tu donc morfillé ?
        Maluré.
J'ai fait suer un chêne,
    Lirlonfa malurette,
Son auberg j'ai enganté,
    Lirlonfa maluré,

Son auberg et sa toquante,
  Lirlonfa malurette,
Et ses attach's de cés,
  Lirlonfa maluré.

Et ces attach's de cés,
    Maluré.
Ma largu' part pour Versailles,
  Lirlonfa malurette,
Aux pieds d'sa majesté,
  Lirlonfa maluré.
Elle lui fonce un babillard,
  Lirlonfa malurette,
Pour m'faire défourrailler,
  Lirlonfa maluré.

Pour m'faire défourrailler,
    Maluré.
Ah! si j'en défourraille,
  Lirlonfa malurette,
Ma largue j'entiferai,
  Lirlonfa maluré.
J'li ferai porter fontange,
  Lirlonfa malurette,
Et souliers galuchés,
  Lirlonfa maluré.

Et souliers galuchés,
    Maluré.
Mais grand dabe qui s'fâche,
  Lirlonfa malurette,
Dit : Par mon caloquet,
  Lirlonfa maluré,
J'li ferai danser une danse,
  Lirlonfa malurette,
Où il n'y a pas de plancher,
  Lirlonfa maluré.

I did not, could not listen to any more of it. The
sense, half-revealed, half-hidden, of this horrible
lament; the struggle of the brigand with the watch,
the thief whom he meets and despatches to his wife
with the ghastly message: " I have killed a man and'
am arrested " (*j'ai fait suer un chêne, et je suis enfourraillé*[1]); the woman, who rushes off to Versailles with her petition, and his Majesty, who loses
his temper and threatens to make the culprit " dance
a dance where there is no floor ; " and all this sung
to the sweetest tune by the sweetest voice that ever
lulled a man to sleep!

I was crushed and heart-broken. It was a repulsive thing to hear those shocking words come from
those fresh, rosy lips. It was like the slime of a
snail upon a lovely flower.

I do not know how to describe my sensation ; I
was wounded and soothed at the same time. The,
patois of the den and the galleys, that grotesque,
barbarous lingo, that disgusting *argot*, uttered by
a maiden's voice, a lovely mean between a child's
voice and a woman's, — all those distorted, ill-made
words sung and trilled with exquisite expression !

Ah ! what an infamous thing a prison is ! There
is a poison there which vitiates everything. Everything within the walls is blighted, even the song of
a girl of fifteen. You find a bird there, — he has
mud upon his wings ; you pick a lovely flower, and
inhale its odor, — it stinks.

[1] Literally — I have made an oak sweat, and am covered.

XVII.

Oh! if I had escaped, how I would have run across the fields!

But no, it would never do to run. That attracts attention and arouses suspicion. On the contrary, I must walk slowly, with head erect, and singing. I must try to get an old blue smock frock with red figures. That would disguise me perfectly. All the market-gardeners in the suburbs wear them.

I know a clump of trees near Arcueil alongside a swamp, where I used to go and fish for bull-frogs with my comrades every Thursday when I was at college. I could hide there until nightfall. Then I would resume my journey. I would go to Vin-cennes. No, the river would prevent me. I would go to Arpajon. It would be much better to go Saint-Germain way, and so to Havre, and sail for America — But no matter! I reach Longjumeau. A gendarme meets me, and asks for my passport. I am lost!

Ah! wretched dreamer, first batter down the three-foot wall which holds you fast! Death! death!

When I think that I came here to Bicêtre when I was a child, to look at the great well and the madmen!

XVIII.

WHILE I was writing this last, my lamp burned pale; the day had come; the clock on the chapel struck six —

What does this mean? The turnkey on guard just entered my dungeon, removed his cap, saluted me, apologized for disturbing me, and asked me, softening his harsh voice as well as he could, what I would like for breakfast.

I shivered from head to foot. Can it be to-day?

XIX.

IT *is* to-day !

The warden of the prison has been in person to pay me a visit. He asked me what he could do for my comfort or convenience; he expressed a hope that I had no complaint to make of him or his subordinates; he asked with much interest about my health, and how I had passed the night. When he took his leave he called me *Monsieur.*

It must be to-day !

XX.

THE jailer does not think that I have any reason
to complain of him or his under-jailers. He is
right. It would be wrong for me to complain.
They have done their duty; they have kept close
watch upon me, and in addition they have been po-
lite to me at my arrival and my departure. Ought I
not to be content?

The good jailer, with his benign smile, his hon-
ied words, his eye which fawns upon you and
watches you at the same moment, and his great,
coarse hands, is the incarnation of the prison, — he
is Bicêtre made man. Everything about me is
prison; I find the prison in every guise, — in human
guise as well as in the guise of bolt or bar. This
wall is the prison in stone; this door is the prison
in wood; these keepers are the prison in flesh and
bone. The prison is an awful sort of creature, complete, indivisible, half-building, half-man. I am its
prey; it seizes me, and winds all its folds about me.
It encompasses me with its granite walls, secures me
with its iron locks, and keeps watch on me with its
jailer's eyes.

Ah! wretched creature that I am! What will become of me? what do they mean to do with me?

XXI.

I AM calm now. All is over, and well over. I am relieved from the horrible anxiety which resulted from the warden's visit. For, I confess, I still had some hope. Now, thank God, hope is at end.

This is what happened : —

Just as the clock was striking half-past six, — no, it was quarter to seven, — the door of my cell opened. An old man with white hair, in a brown redingote, came in. He opened his redingote. I saw a cassock and a neck-band. It was a priest.

He was not the prison chaplain. He is a man of sinister appearance.

He sat down opposite me with a kindly smile; then he shook his head, and raised his eyes to heaven, that is to say, to the arched ceiling of the dungeon. I understood him.

"My son," he said, "are you prepared ?"

I answered in a feeble voice : —

"I am not prepared, but I am ready."

Meanwhile a mist came before my eyes, an icy sweat broke out over my whole body, I felt my temples throbbing as if they would burst, and there was a confused ringing in my ears.

While I was swaying about on my chair as if I were falling asleep, the good old man was speaking.

At least, so it seemed to me, and I think I can remember seeing his lips move, his hands wave, and his eyes glisten.

The door opened a second time. The noise of the bolts roused me from my stupor, and interrupted his discourse. A gentleman in a black coat came in, accompanied by the warden, and bowed low to me. This man had in his expression something of the perfunctory, official melancholy of mutes at a funeral. He had a roll of paper in his hand.

"Monsieur," he said to me with a courteous smile, "I am an usher from the king's court at Paris. I have the honor to be the bearer of a communication to you from Monsieur le Procureur du Roi."

The first shock had passed away. All my presence of mind had returned.

"It was Monsieur le Procureur du Roi, was it not," I rejoined, "who demanded my head so earnestly? It's a great honor to me that he should write to me. I hope that my death will give him the greatest pleasure, for it would be very hard for me to think that it was a matter of indifference to him, when he was so ardent in seeking it."

I said all this, and added in a firm voice : —

"Read on, monsieur."

He began to read a long screed, with a rising inflection at the end of every line, and hesitating in the middle of every word. It was the formal dismissal of my appeal.

"The sentence will be executed to-day on the Place de Grève," he added when the reading was at an end, — without taking his eyes from the stamped

paper. " We start at half-past seven precisely for the
Conciergerie. My dear monsieur, will you have the
extreme kindness to follow me ? "

For some moments I had not been listening. The
warden was talking with the priest ; the usher had
his eyes glued to his paper ; I was looking at the door
which was left half-open. Ah ! unlucky wretch ! four
fusileers in the corridor !

The usher repeated his question, and this time he
looked at me.

" When you choose, monsieur," I said, — " at your
convenience."

He bowed, and said : —

" I shall have the honor of coming to fetch you in
half an hour."

With that they left me alone.

Some means of flight, oh, my God ! — any means
under heaven ! I must escape ! I must ! at once !
by the door, by the window, through the roof, even
though I leave some of my flesh on the timbers !

O fury ! demons ! the curse of hell ! Months I
must have to cut through this wall with good tools,
and I have not a nail or an hour !

XXII.

HERE I am, *transferred*, as the report has it.

But the journey is worth the trouble of describing.

Half-past seven was striking when the usher appeared again at the door of my cell.

"Monsieur," he said, "I am waiting for you." Alas! he and others besides!

I rose, and took one step; it seemed to me as if I could not take a second, my head was so heavy and my legs so weak. However, I made a mighty effort, and walked along with a reasonably firm step. Before leaving my cell, I cast a last glance around. I loved it, do you know? And then, too, I left it empty and open, which gives a dungeon a singular appearance.

It will not remain so long, however. They expect an occupant for it this evening, so the turnkeys said, — a man whom the Assize Court is on the point of transforming into a condemned man at this moment.

At a bend in the corridor the chaplain joined us. He had been breakfasting. As we left the jail the director grasped my hand affectionately, and added four veterans to my escort.

As I passed the door of the infirmary an old man at the point of death cried : " Au revoir!"

We reached the courtyard. I breathed the fresh air, and it did me good.

We walked but a short distance in the air. A carriage drawn by post horses was standing in the outer courtyard, — the same carriage in which I rode to Bicêtre. It is a sort of cabriolet, oblong in shape, divided into two sections by a transverse grating of wire of such fine mesh that you would say it was knitted. Each of the two sections has a door. The whole is so black and filthy and dusty that the pauper's hearse is a state carriage in comparison.

Before burying myself in this two-wheeled tomb I cast a glance into the courtyard, — one of those despairing glances before which it seems as if stone walls must crumble. It was a little square planted with trees, and was more crowded with spectators than it had been for the galley-slaves. A crowd already !

As on the day that the chain-gang started for Toulon, a fine, cold rain was falling ; it is falling still as I write, and will doubtless fall all day, and last longer than I shall. The roads were washed out, and the yard was full of mud and water. I enjoyed seeing the crowd wallowing in the mire.

The usher and a gendarme entered the forward compartment ; the priest, a gendarme, and myself, the other. Four mounted gendarmes surrounded the carriage. Thus there were eight men for one, not including the postilion.

While I was climbing in, a blear-eyed old woman exclaimed : —

"I like this better than the chain-gang."

I can imagine it. It is a spectacle which one

takes in more easily at a glance, it can be seen more quickly. It is quite as fine a sight, and more convenient. There is nothing to distract your mind. There is only one man, and in that one man's soul as much misery as in all the convicts at once. That is more diluted; this is concentrated liquor, and much more highly flavored.

The carriage started. It passed with a dull rumble under the arch of the main gateway, turned into the avenue, and the heavy gates of Bicêtre clanged to behind it. I realized that I was being taken away, but stupidly, like a man in a lethargy, who hears that he is to be buried, but can neither move nor cry out. I listened dreamily to the bells about the necks of the post horses ringing by jerks as if they had the hiccoughs, the iron-shod wheels rumbling over the pavement, or thumping against the body as they changed from one rut to another, the galloping hoof-beats of the gendarmes' horses around the carriage, and the cracking of the postilion's whip. It all seemed to me like a whirlwind which was whirling me away.

Through the bars placed across a round hole in front of me as I sat, my eyes were fixed mechanically upon the inscription in large letters over the great gate of Bicêtre: —

"HOSPICE DE LA VIEILLESSE!"[1]

"So!" I said to myself, "it seems that there are people who live to grow old there."

As one often does between sleep and waking, I

[1] Asylum for the Aged.

turned that idea over and over in my grief-benumbed
mind. Suddenly the carriage turned from the avenue
into the high-road, and the view through the peep-
hole changed. The towers of Nôtre Dame appeared
in that frame, seen but indistinctly in the bluish haze
of Paris. On the instant the current of my thought
also changed. I had become a mere machine like
the carriage. The thought of Bicêtre was succeeded
by the thought of the towers of Nôtre Dame.

"Those who are on the tower where the flag is
will have a fine view of it," I said to myself with a
stupid smile.

I think it was just then that the priest began to
talk to me. I meekly permitted him to talk on. I
already had in my ears the rumbling of the wheels,
the galloping of the horses, and the postilion's whip.
This was simply one noise more.

I was listening silently to the monotonous flow
of words, which lulled my thoughts to sleep like the
plashing of a fountain, and passed before my mind,
always different, yet always the same, like the
gnarled elms along the road, when the quick, jerky
tones of the usher, who was sitting in the forward
compartment, abruptly roused me.

"Well, Monsieur l'Abbé!" he said, almost gayly,
"do you know any news?"

He turned to the priest as he spoke.

The priest, made deaf by the noise of the wheels,
kept on talking to me, and made no reply.

"Hé! hé!" continued the usher, raising his voice
so as to drown the noise, "what an infernal rattle-
trap!"

Infernal!   In good sooth, yes.

"It's the jolting, of course," he went on; "it's impossible to hear.   What was I saying?   Be good enough to tell me what I was saying, Monsieur l'Abbé.   Oh, have you heard the great news at Paris to-day?"

I started as if he were speaking of me.

"No," said the priest, who heard him at last. "I had no time to read the papers this morning.   I shall see them this evening.   When I am engaged like this for all day, I tell the concierge to keep my papers, and I read them when I return."

"Nonsense!" rejoined the usher, "it isn't possible that you don't know this, — the sensation of Paris! this morning's news!"

I joined in the conversation.

"I think I know it."

The usher looked at me.

"You! indeed!   If that is so, what do you think of it?"

"You are inquisitive," I retorted.

"Why so, monsieur?   Every one has his own political opinion.   I esteem you too highly to believe that you have none.   As for myself, I am altogether in favor of the reorganization of the National Guard.   I was sergeant of my company, and 'faith, it was very pleasant."

"I didn't suppose that that was what you referred to," I broke in.

"What then, pray   You said that you knew the news."

"I was speaking of something else, which also engrosses the attention of Paris to-day."

The idiot did not understand; his curiosity was
aroused.

"Other news?   Where the devil could you have
heard the news?   What is it, my dear sir, in God's
name?   Do you know what it is, Monsieur l'Abbé?
Are you better posted than I?   Tell me, I beg you,
what is it about?   Come, I love to hear news.   I tell
it to Monsieur le Président, and it amuses him."

And so does much other silly stuff.   He turned
first to the priest, then to me, and I made no other
reply than to shrug my shoulders.

"Well," he said to me, "what are you thinking
about, pray?"

"I am thinking," I replied, "that I shall have
ceased to think this evening."

"Ah! that indeed!" he rejoined.   "Go to, you
are too gloomy.   M. Castaing talked.

"I escorted M. Papavoine, too," he resumed, after
a pause; "he wore his otter-skin cap, and smoked
his cigar.   The young men from La Rochelle talked
only to one another.   But they talked."

Again he paused, and began again :—

"Idiots! fanatics!   They acted as if they held the
whole world in contempt.   But when we come to
you, I think you are too pensive by half, young
man."

"Young man!" I retorted, "I am older than you;
every quarter of an hour that passes makes me a
year older."

He turned around and stared blankly at me for a
moment, then began to laugh sneeringly.

"Ha, ha! you are joking.   Older than I?   I
might be your grandfather!"

"I am not joking," I said gravely.

He opened his snuff-box.

"Come, don't be angry, dear monsieur; take a pinch of snuff, and don't bear me a grudge."

"Don't be alarmed; I sha'n't have long to bear it."

As I spoke, his snuff-box, which he was passing to me, came in contact with the screen which separated us. An opportune jolt made the contact so violent that the open box fell at the gendarme's feet.

"Cursed screen!" exclaimed the usher. "Well! am I not unlucky?" he said to me; "I have lost all my snuff!"

"I am losing more than you," I replied with a smile.

He undertook to pick up the snuff, grumbling between his teeth:—

"More than I! that's easy to say. But no snuff this side of Paris! it's terrible!"

The chaplain thereupon said a few consoling words to him, and I do not know whether it was due to absent-mindedness, but I certainly thought he was going on with the exhortation of which I had the beginning. Little by little the priest and the usher entered into conversation; I let them talk at will, and gave myself up to reflection.

As we approached the barrier, I was still deeply absorbed doubtless, but it seemed to me that Paris was making more noise than usual.

The carriage stopped a moment at the custom-house. The customs officers made their examination. If it had been a sheep or an ox being taken to the slaughter-house, it would have been necessary to give them money, but a human head pays no duty. We passed through.

After crossing the boulevard, the carriage plunged in among the old winding streets of the Faubourg Saint-Marceau and the Cité, which twist about, and cross this way and that like the thousand paths of a labyrinth. On the pavements of these narrow streets the rumbling of the carriage became so deafening and incessant that I could hear no other of the outside noises. When I looked out through the little square peep-hole, I fancied that the flood of passers-by stopped to look at the carriage, and that swarms of children were running along behind. It seemed to me also as if I could see from time to time a man or an old woman in rags, sometimes the two together, standing on the street-corners, holding in their hands a parcel of printed sheets which the people struggled to get hold of, and opening their mouths as if to shout.

Half-past eight was striking on the Palace clock when we drove into the courtyard of the Conciergerie. The sight of the long flight of steps, the black chapel, and the ominous wickets, froze my blood. When the carriage stopped I thought that the beating of my heart would stop too.

I summoned all my strength of will; the door opened as quickly as a lightning-flash; I jumped down from the wheeled dungeon, and strode hastily under the arch between two lines of soldiers. A crowd was already collected to see me pass.

XXIII.

So long as I was walking through the public corridors of the Palais de Justice, I felt almost free, and at ease; but all my resolution abandoned me when I began to pass through low doors, secret stairways, interior lobbies, long, stifling, dark corridors, where none enter save them who condemn, and them who are condemned.

The usher still accompanied me. The priest had left me, to come again in two hours. He had business to attend to.

They took me to the office of the warden, and the usher placed me in his charge. It was an exchange. The warden begged him to wait a moment, saying that he had some game to turn over to him to be taken at once to Bicêtre by return carriage. Doubtless it was the man condemned to-day, who is to lie to-night upon the bunch of straw which I had not time to use up.

"Very well," said the usher. "I will wait; we can draw up both reports at once; it comes about very nicely."

Meanwhile they deposited me in a little closet adjoining the office. There they left me alone, securely locked in.

I have no idea what I was thinking about, nor how long I had been there, when a loud, strident laugh in my ear roused me abruptly from my revery.

I looked up with a start. I was no longer alone in the cell. A man stood beside me, — a man of about fifty-five, of medium height, wrinkled and bent, with grizzly hair and beard ; his legs and arms were stocky and powerful ; he had a cunning expression in his bleared eyes, and a bitter, sneering smile upon his face ; he was filthy, half-clothed in rags, and repulsive to look upon.

It would seem that the door had opened, vomited him in, and closed again, without attracting my attention. If death might only come so !

The man and I looked each other in the eye for a few seconds, — he, with a prolongation of his laugh which resembled a death-rattle, and I, half-wondering, and half-afraid.

" Who are you ? " I said at length.

" That's a devil of a question ! " he retorted. " A *frianche.*"

" A *frianche !* What does that mean ? "

This question seemed to redouble his mirth.

" It means," he cried, in the midst of a roar of laughter, " that the *taule* (executioner) will drop my *sorbonne* (head) into the basket in six weeks, as he is going to do with your *tronche* (head) in six hours. Ha ! ha ! you seem to understand now."

Indeed I had turned pale and my hair was standing on end. It was the man just sentenced to death, the one they were expecting at Bicêtre, — my heir !

He went on : —

" What's the matter ? This is my story. I am the son of a good sort of fellow. It was a shame that Charlot (the executioner) should take a fancy

one day to tie his cravat.   It was in the days when
the gallows reigned, by the grace of God.   At six, I
had no father nor mother ; in the summer I turned
handsprings along the side of the road, to induce
some one to throw me a sou from the post-chaise
doors ; in winter I went barefooted in the mud, blow-
ing on my purple fingers; you could see my legs
through my trousers.   At nine I began to use my
louches (hands), now and then I emptied a *fouillouse*
(pocket), or *filais une pelure* (stole a cloak) ; at ten I
was a *marlou* (pickpocket).   Then I made acquaint-
ances, and at seventeen I was a *grinche* (robber).   I
broke into a *boutanche* (shop).   I made a false *tour-
nante* (key).   They caught me.   I was of age, and
they sent me *to row in the little navy.*[1]   It 's a hard
life at the galleys: to sleep on a board, drink clear
water, eat black bread, drag around a cannon-ball
that 's of no use ; club-strokes and sun-strokes.
Added to all that, you are shaved, and I had beautiful
chestnut hair !   No matter ! I did my time.   Fifteen
years, that takes it out of a man !   I was thirty-three
years old.   One fine morning they gave me a ticket
for the coach and sixty-six francs I had saved in my
fifteen years at the galleys, working sixteen hours a
day, thirty days a month, and twelve months a year.
All the same I determined to be an honest man with
my sixty-six francs, and I had more noble sentiments
under my rags than there are under *une serpillière de
ratichon* (an abbé's cassock).   But the devil take their
passport !   it was yellow, and ' discharged convict '
was written at the top.   I had to show it wherever

[1] To the galleys.

I went, and to present it every week to the mayor of
the town where they forced me to *tapiquer* (live).
A fine recommendation that ! — a galley-slave ! I
frightened people, the little children ran away from
me, and doors were shut in my face. No one would
give me work. I ate up my sixty-six francs. I had
to live somehow. I showed my strong arms ; I
offered to work for fifteen sous a day, for ten, for five.
No. What was I to do ? One day I was hungry ; I
put my elbow through the window of a bakery ;
I grabbed a loaf and the baker grabbed me. I did n't
eat the bread, but I got the galleys for life, and three
letters branded on my shoulder. I 'll show you, if
you choose. That 's what they call the *récidive*.[1] So
there I was, a *cheval de retour* (returned to the
galleys). They took me back to Toulon ; this time
they put me with the green bonnets.[2] There was no
way out of it but escape. To do that I had only
three walls to cut through and two chains to cut, and
I had a nail. I escaped. They fired the alarm gun ;
for we are dressed in red like the cardinals at Rome,
and they fire the cannon when we take leave. Their
powder went to the sparrows. This time I had no
passport, but no money either. I fell in with comrades who had also done their time, or broken their
chains. Their *coire* (leader) proposed to me to join
them ; *on faisait la grande soulasse sur le trimar*
(they were robbing and murdering on the high-roads).
I accepted, and I went to work killing for a living.
Sometimes it was a diligence, sometimes a post-chaise,
sometimes a cattle-dealer on horseback. We took

---

[1] Penalty for the second offence.   [2] Life convicts.

his money, let the beast or the team go where they chose, and buried the man under a tree, taking care that his feet did n't stick out ; and then we danced on the grave so that the ground would n't look as if it had been dug up lately. I grew old in that business, lying in the hedges, sleeping under the stars, hunted from wood to wood, but free at least, and my own man. Everything has an end, and that as well as everything else. The *marchands de lacets* (gendarmes) took us by the collar one fine night. My *fanandels* (companions) escaped ; but I, the oldest of all, remained in the claws of the cats with gold lace on their hats. They brought me here. I have already climbed all the rungs of the ladder but one. Whether I stole a handkerchief or killed a man, it was all one for me then ; there was one more *récidive* to apply to me. There was nothing left for me but to go through the hands of the *faucheur* (executioner). It was a short story with me. Faith, I am beginning to grow old, and to be good for nothing. My father *married the widow*,[1] and I am about to withdraw to the *abbaye de Mont'-à-Regret* (the guillotine). That's the whole of it, comrade."

I listened to him, still in a sort of stupor. He began to laugh louder than when he began, and offered to take my hand. I recoiled.

"Friend," he said, "you don't seem to be very brave. Don't play the *sinvre · devant la carline* (coward in the face of death). It is an ugly feeling when you go to the *placarde* (Place de Grève), but it's soon over, you see. I'd like to be there to

---

[1] Was hanged.

show you how to fall. Ten thousand gods! I 've
a mind not to appeal, if they 'll *me faucher* (cut off
my head) with yours to-day. The same priest will
do for both of us ; I 'd as soon have what you leave.
I 'm a good fellow, you see. Hein ! say, what shall
it be, — friendship ? "

He came a step nearer to me.

" Monsieur," I replied, pushing him away, " I 'm
obliged to you."

A fresh burst of laughter greeted my reply.

" Ha ! ha ! monsieur, you are a marquis ! He 's a
marquis ! "

" My friend," I said, interrupting him, " I need
time to reflect ; leave me."

The gravity of my tone made him suddenly
thoughtful. He shook his almost bald gray head ;
then he muttered between his teeth, digging his nails
into his hairy chest, which his shirt left bare :

" I understand : the *sanglier* [1] (priest) of course ! "

After a few moments of silence he began again.

" Look ye," he said, almost timidly, " you are a
marquis, that 's very fine ; but you have a handsome
coat there which won't do you much good. The
taule will take it. Give it to me, and I will sell it
and buy tobacco."

I took off my coat and handed it to him. He
clapped his hands in childish glee. Then, seeing
that I was shivering in my shirt, he said : —

" You are cold, monsieur, put on this ; it rains,
and you will get wet ; and then, too, you must make
a decent appearance on the tumbril."

---

[1] Literally — wild-boar.

As he spoke, he removed his coarse, gray linen waistcoat, and put my arms through the sleeves. I made no resistance.

After that I stood up and leaned against the wall. I should not know how to describe the effect the man produced upon me. He was making an examination of the coat I gave him, and was exclaiming with delight every instant.

"The pockets are all new; the collar is n't worn at all! I shall get at least fifteen francs for it. What luck! a supply of tobacco for my six weeks!"

The door opened once more. They came for both of us; for me, to take me to the room where the doomed await the hour of doom; for him, to take him to Bicêtre. He took his place laughingly in the centre of the squad which was to have him in charge, and said to the gendarmes: —

"Ah, ça! don't make a mistake; Monsieur and I have changed skins, but don't take me in his place. The devil! that would never do, now that I have something to get tobacco with!"

27

XXIV.

THE old villain took my coat, — for I did not give it to him, — and left me this disgusting rag, his old waistcoat. What shall I look like?

I let him take my coat, not from indifference or charity, — no, but because he was stronger than I. If I had refused he would have beaten me with his great fists.

Ah, yes, charity! I was filled with evil thoughts. I would have liked to be able to strangle him with my hands, the old thief! — to trample him under my feet!

My heart feels as if it were overflowing with rage and bitterness. I believe that my gall-bladder has burst. Death makes a man wicked.

XXV.

THEY have put me in a cell where there is nothing but the four walls, with many bars at the window and many bolts on the door, it is needless to
say.

I asked for a table, a chair, and writing materials.
They brought me all of them.

Then I asked for a bed. The turnkey looked at
me in utter amazement, as if to say: " What for ? "

However, they put a bed in one corner. But at
the same time a gendarme took up his quarters in
what they call my *chamber*. Are they afraid I will
strangle myself with the mattress ?

XXVI.

It is ten o'clock.

O my poor, poor little girl! six hours more and I shall be dead! I shall have become something unclean, to be displayed on the cold operating table in lecture rooms: a head to be ground up on one side, and a trunk to be dissected on the other; then they will fill a coffin with what is left, and the whole will be carted off to Clamart.

That is what they are going to do with your father, — these men, no one of whom hates me, but all pity me, and might save me if they chose. They are going to kill me. Do you understand that, Marie? — kill me in cold blood, with pomp and circumstance, for the good of society. Ah! great God!

Poor little one! your father, who loved you so dearly; your father, who kissed your sweet white neck, who passed his hand unceasingly through your silky curls, who took your pretty, chubby face in his hands, who trotted you on his knees, and in the evening put your little hands together to pray!

Who is there to do all that now? Who is there to love you? All the children of your age have fathers, except you. How, my darling, will you learn to go without your New Year's gifts, your lovely toys and sweetmeats and kisses? How will you learn to go without food and drink, unhappy orphan?

Oh! if those jurors had but seen my pretty little Marie, they would have realized that they must not kill the father of a child of three.

And when she grows up, if she lives to grow up, what will become of her? Her father will be a by-word among the people of Paris. She will blush for me and for my name; she will be despised, avoided, vilified on my account, who love her with all the love of my heart. O my little Marie, my darling child! Is it true that you will think of me with shame and horror?

Miserable wretch! what a crime did I commit, and what a crime I am making society commit!

Oh! is it really true that I am to die before the close of day? Is it true that this is I? The dull outcry which I hear without, the flood of joyous, happy people, who are already hurrying to the quays, the gendarmes making ready in their barracks, the black-robed priest, the other man with the red hands, — it is all for me! it is I who am to die! I, who am here, who live and move and breathe, who am sitting at this table, which is like any other table, and might as well be elsewhere, — I, in short, this I, whom I touch and feel, and whose clothing I hold in my hand!

XXVII.

IF I only knew how it is done, and in what way one dies; but it is horrible, I know nothing about it.

The very name of the thing is frightful, and I cannot comprehend how I have been able heretofore to write it and speak it.

The combination of the ten letters, their appearance, their physiognomy is well calculated to cause terrifying thoughts, and the wretched physician who invented the thing had a name of evil omen.

The image which I couple with the hideous word is vague and indeterminate, and so much the more forbidding on that account. Each syllable is like a part of the machine. I build and tear down the awful structure in my imagination every moment.

I dare not ask a question concerning it, but it is a fearful thing not to know what it is, nor what to expect. It would seem that there is a lever, and that they make you lie on your stomach— Ah! my hair will turn white before my head falls!

XXVIII.

I DID see it once, however.

I was passing through the Place de Grève one day, in a carriage, about eleven in the morning. Suddenly the carriage stopped.

I put my head out of the window. There was a great crowd which filled the square and the quay, and men, women, and children were standing on the parapet. Above their heads I could see a sort of platform of red wood, which three men were building.

A man was to be executed that day, and they were preparing the machine. I turned my head away before I fairly saw it. Beside the carriage a woman was saying to a child: —

" The knife does n't run smoothly, and they are going to grease the grooves with a candle-end."

That 's what they are doing to-day probably. Eleven o'clock is just striking. They are greasing the grooves, no doubt.

Ah ! this time I shall not turn my head away, poor wretch !

XXIX.

Oh, my pardon! my pardon! perhaps they will grant my pardon! The king has nothing against me. Let some one go for my advocate! The advocate, quickly! I will take the galleys. Five years at the galleys, and let it go at that — or twenty years — or life and the red-hot iron. But spare my life!

A convict still walks, you know, and goes and comes, and sees the sunlight.

XXX.

THE priest has returned.

He has white hair, a very gentle expression, and a kind and venerable face ; he is in truth, a most excellent and charitable man. This morning I saw him empty his purse into the prisoners' hands. How happens it that his voice has no emotional quality, and arouses no emotion ? Why is it that he has said nothing to me which appeals to my intellect or to my heart ?

This morning my mind was wandering. I hardly heard what he said. And yet his words seemed useless to me, and made no impression upon me ; they rolled off me, as the cold rain rolls down yonder window-pane.

But when he came in just now the sight of him did me good. Of all mankind he is the only one who is still a man so far as I am concerned, I said to myself. And thereupon I was seized with a burning thirst for kindly, consoling words.

We sat down, he on the chair, and I on the bed.

" My son," he began.

That word opened my heart.

" My son, do you believe in God ? "

" Yes, father," I replied.

" Do you believe in the holy Roman Catholic and Apostolic Church ? "

"Implicitly," I said.

"My son, your bearing seems to me to indicate doubt."

Thereupon he began to talk. He talked a long while; he used many words, and when he thought he had said enough, he rose and looked at me, inquiringly, for the first time since he began his harangue.

"Well?" he said.

I protest that I had listened to him, eagerly at first, then with deep attention, and at last, devoutly.

I also rose.

"Monsieur," said I, "leave me alone, I beg you."

"When shall I return?" he asked.

"I will send for you."

He went out then without saying anything further, but shaking his head as if he were saying to himself:

"An impious fellow!"

No; low as I have fallen, I am not impious, and God is my witness that I believe in him. But what did the old man say to me? Not a word of deep feeling, nothing torn from the soul, nothing which came from his heart straight to mine, not a word directly from him to me. On the contrary, a mass of vague, colorless phrases applicable to anybody at any time; emphatic where depth of reasoning was demanded, and prosy where he should have been simple; a sort of sentimental sermon and theological monody. Here and there, a Latin quotation, — Saint Augustine, Saint Gregory, or God knows who. And then he seemed to be reciting a lesson he had recited twenty times before, rehearsing a theme which he

knew so well that he had forgotten it. Not a look
of the eye, not an inflection of the voice, not a gesture with the hands.

And how could it be otherwise? This priest is the
official chaplain of the prison. His business is to
comfort and exhort, and he lives by it. The convicts and the men condemned to death are the tar-
gets for his eloquence. He confesses them and helps
them, because it's his business. He has grown old
accompanying men to their death. For a long,
long while he has been accustomed to things which
make other men shudder; his hair, well sprinkled
with white, no longer stands on end; the galleys and
the scaffold are every-day matters for him; he is
blasé. Probably he has it all written down in a
book, one page for the galley-slaves, another for
those condemned to death. They notify him the
night before that there is some one to whom he is to
administer consolation on the following day at such
an hour. He inquires whether it's a galley-slave or
the other, and reads over the proper page; then he
makes his visit. In this way it happens that those
who go to Toulon and those who go to the Grève
are commonplace mortals in his eyes, and he is very
commonplace in his dealings with them.

Oh! pray go and find, instead of him, any young
vicar, or old curate in the nearest parish, it matters
not who he is; catch him as he sits in his chimney
corner, reading his book, and expecting nothing of
the sort, and say to him : —

"There is a man who is going to die, and you must
come and console him. You must be there when

they bind his hands, when they cut off his hair; you
must mount the tumbril with him, with your crucifix
to hide the executioner; you must be jolted along
over the pavements with him to the Place de Grève;
you must go with him through the bloodthirsty
mob; you must embrace him at the foot of the scaffold, and remain there until the head is on one side
and the body on the other."

Then, bring him to me as I sit here panting and
shivering from head to foot; throw me into his arms,
or on the floor at his knees; and he will weep, and
we will weep together, and he will be eloquent, and
I shall be comforted, and my heart will pour out its
agony into his, and he will take my soul, and I will
take his God.

But of what service is this old man to me? What
am I to him? An individual of the species unfortunate, a shade of the kind of which he has already
seen so many, a unit to add to the total number of
executions.

Perhaps I am wrong to hold aloof from him thus;
it is he who is good, and I who am bad. Alas! it is
not my fault. It is my breath, the breath of a condemned man, that spoils and withers everything it
touches.

They have just brought me food; they thought
that I must need it, — a very dainty and delicate
repast; a chicken, I believe, and something else.
Oh, well! I tried to eat; but the first mouthful fell
back on the plate, it tasted so bitter and offensive.

XXXI.

A MAN came in a moment ago, with his hat on his head; he glanced carelessly at me, then opened a foot rule, and began to measure the stones of the wall, calling off the measurements in a very loud voice.

I asked a gendarme who he was. It seems that he is an assistant-architect employed at the prison.

His curiosity was aroused in regard to me. He exchanged a few words in a low voice with the turnkey who accompanied him, then fixed his eyes upon me for a moment, shook his head with an indifferent air, and began again to take his measurements and call them.

When his work was done he came up to me, and said in his piercing voice : —

"My good friend, this prison will be much improved in six months' time."

The gesture which accompanied his words seemed to add : —

"You won't be here to enjoy it; it's a great pity."

He almost smiled. I thought for a moment that he was going to have a little fun at my expense, as one jokes a young bridegroom on his wedding night.

My gendarme, an old soldier with stripes on his shoulders, took it upon himself to reply.

" Monsieur," he said, " we don't talk so loud in a dead man's room."

The architect took his leave.

I remained behind, like one of the stones he measured.

XXXII.

AFTER that a most absurd thing happened to me.

My kind old gendarme was relieved, and I, selfish ingrate that I am, did not even press his hand. He was replaced by a man with a retreating forehead, the eyes of a calf, and an idiotic face.

However, I took no notice of him. I turned my back to the door, as I sat at my table. I tried to cool my forehead with my hand, and my thoughts kept my mind in a state of confusion.

A light touch on my shoulder made me turn my head. It was the new gendarme; he and I were alone in the room.

He spoke to me, and these are almost exactly the words he used: —

" Criminal, have you a good heart ? "

" No," I said.

My abrupt response seemed to disconcert him. However, he continued, hesitatingly: —

" Men are not wicked just for the pleasure of being so."

" Why not ? " I retorted. " If you have nothing but that to say to me, leave me. What are you coming at ? "

" Pardon me, criminal," he replied. " Just a word. If you could make a poor man happy, and it wouldn't cost you anything, wouldn't you do it ? "

I shrugged my shoulders testily.

"Are you just from Charenton? You select a singular vessel to pour happiness from. The idea of my making anybody happy!"

He lowered his voice, and assumed a mysterious expression, which did not set well on his idiotic features.

"Yes, criminal, yes, happiness and fortune, — I may get all that from you. Look you. I am a poor gendarme. The work is heavy and the pay small; my horse is my own, and it ruins me to keep him. Now I have gone into the lottery to even things up. One must have something to live on. Thus far I have only lacked the lucky numbers to win. I have tried every way to make sure which they are; I always make a mess of it. If I take seventy-six, the prize goes to seventy-seven. It's of no use for me to cultivate them, they don't come up. Patience, please; I am almost done. Now, here's a fine opportunity for me. It seems — I beg your pardon, criminal — that you are to die to-day. It is certain that those who die in this way can tell the lucky numbers in the lottery in advance. Promise me that you will come to-morrow night, — what difference will it make to you? — and give me three winning numbers. What do you say? I am not afraid of ghosts, never fear! Here's my address: Popincourt Barracks, Staircase A., No. 26, at the end of the corridor. You will recognize me, won't you? Come this evening, if it's more convenient for you."

I should have scorned to answer the fool, if a mad hope had not passed through my mind. In the desperate position I am in, it seems at times as if one could break his chains with a hair.

"Listen," I said to him, playing the comedian as far as a man can who has death staring him in the face; "I can make you richer than the king, I can put you in the way to win millions, — on one condition."

He opened his stupid eyes to their fullest extent.

"What is it? what is it? — anything to please you, my criminal."

"Instead of three numbers, I promise you four. Change clothes with me."

"If that's all you want!" he cried, beginning to unfasten his coat.

I rose from my chair. I watched his every movement with beating heart. I already saw the doors opening before the gendarme's uniform, and the square and the street and the Palais de Justice behind me!

But he turned to me hesitatingly.

"Ah! it's not to help you get away from here?"

I realized that all was lost. However, I made one last effort, — a useless, insensate effort!

"To be sure," I said, "but your fortune is made — "

He cut me short.

"No, no! What about my numbers? To have them win, you must be dead."

I had fallen back on my chair, speechless and more despairing and hopeless than ever.

XXXIII.

I closed my eyes, put my hands over them, and tried to forget the present in the past. When I am dreaming thus, the memories of my childhood and my youth come to my mind one by one, — tranquil, smiling, like islets of bright flowers in the gulf of confused, dark thoughts with which my brain is whirling.

I see myself a child once more, a light-hearted, red-cheeked schoolboy, playing and running, and shouting with my brothers in the broad, green paths of the uncultivated garden in which my early years were passed, formerly the abode of a community of nuns, overlooked by the frowning dome of the Val de Grace.

And then I see myself four years later, still a child, but already developing a dreamy, passionate nature. There was a little maid in the lonely garden.

The little Spaniard, with her great eyes and long hair, her golden-brown complexion, her red lips and rosy cheeks, — Pepa, the Andalusian maid, then fourteen years old.

Our mothers told us to go and run about together; we walked instead.

They told us to play, and we talked, — children of the same age, but not of the same sex.

But a year later we were running and fighting together. I fought with Pepita for the finest apple on the tree ; I struck her in a dispute about a bird's-nest. She wept ; I said, " I 'm glad I did it ! " and we both ran off to complain to our mothers, who told us aloud that we were wrong, but whispered that we were right.

Now she is leaning on my arm, and I am proud and excited. We are walking slowly and talking in low tones. She drops her handkerchief; I pick it up. Our hands tremble when they touch each other. She talks about the little birds, about the star over our heads, about the sun setting redly behind the trees, or about her schoolmates, her dress, and her ribbons. We say innocent things and both blush furiously. The little maid has become a young woman.

That evening — it was in summer-time — we were under the chestnuts at the end of the garden. After one of the long pauses which were a common incident of our walks, she took her hand from my arm, and said : —

" Let us run ! "

And she set off before me, with her figure as slender as a bee's waist, and her little feet, which raised her dress above her ankles as she ran. I followed her ; she ran the faster. The wind now and again lifted her black cape, and let me see her smooth, brown flesh.

I was beside myself. I overtook her beside the old ruined well ; I seized her around the waist, by right of conquest, and made her sit down upon a bit of turf. She did not resist. She was out of breath and was smiling. But I was very serious, and I gazed into her black eyes through their long, black lashes.

"Sit down there," she said. "It is still very light; let us read something. Have you a book?"

I had in my pocket the second volume of Spallanzani's "Voyages." I opened it at random and sat down beside her; she leaned her shoulder against mine, and we began to read the same page, each for himself, beneath our breaths. She was always compelled to wait for me before turning the leaf. My mind worked much more slowly than hers.

"Have you finished?" she would say, almost before I had begun.

Meanwhile our heads were touching, my hair and hers were mingled together, and suddenly our lips met.

When we were ready to continue our reading, the stars were shining bright.

"Oh! mamma, mamma," she said, when we returned, "if you knew how we ran!"

I held my peace.

"You don't say anything," said my mother; "you seem sad."

I had paradise in my heart.

It was an evening I shall remember all my life. All my life!

XXXIV.

SOME hour just struck, — I don't know what; I heard the clock indistinctly. It seems to me that I have an organ in my ears; it is the buzzing of my last thoughts.

At this supreme moment, as I go back over the past, my crime fills me with horror; but I would be glad to feel even more repentant than I do. My remorse was greater before my conviction; since then, it has seemed as if I had no room for any other than thoughts of death. However, I would like to be very repentant.

After dreaming a moment of my past life, when I come back to the blow of the knife which is to end it so soon, I shudder as if I had never thought of it before. Oh! my beautiful childhood! my beautiful youth! — gilded stuff of which the ends are soaked in blood! Between those days and the present there is a river of blood; the other's blood and my own.

If any one reads my story hereafter, after so many years of innocence and happiness, they will refuse to credit this last execrable year, which opens with a crime, and closes with an execution; the two will seem so ill-assorted.

And yet, wretched laws and wretched men, I was not bad at heart!

Oh! to die in an hour or two, and to think that on a day like this, only a year ago, I was free and unstained with crime, — that I was taking my autumn walks, wandering under the trees among the falling leaves.

XXXV.

At this very moment there are all about me, in the houses around the Palace and the Place de Grève, and in every part of Paris, men coming and going, talking and laughing, reading the papers, and thinking over their business; merchants buying and selling; young women preparing their dresses for the ball this evening; mothers playing with their children!

XXXVI.

I REMEMBER that one day when I was a child I went to see the great bell of Notre-Dame.

I was giddy from climbing up the dark staircase at a snail's pace, from passing across the frail gallery which connects the two towers, and from looking down at Paris spread out under my feet, when I entered the cage of wood and stone in which the great bell swings, with its tongue that weighs a thousand pounds.

I went forward trembling over the ill-laid boards, gazing from a distance at the bell which is so famous among the children of Paris, noticing not without alarm that the slate-covered sloping roofs which surround the bell were on a level with my feet. Through the interstices I could see the Place du Parvis-Notre-Dame, and the people crawling along like ants.

Suddenly the enormous affair struck the hour; a mighty vibration filled the air and shook the heavy tower. The floor leaped up from the beams. The noise almost overturned me; I staggered, and was on the point of falling, of sliding down upon the sloping roofs. In my terror I lay upon the boards, clinging to them with both hands, speechless, breathless, with the crashing din in my ears, and under my eyes the yawning precipice, with the square at the bottom, where so many men and women were walking quietly to and fro ; and how I envied them !

It seems to me now as if I were still in the bell-tower. I am stunned and dizzy all the time. There is a noise as of ringing bells which fills the cavities of my brain, and I can no longer see, except in the dim distance, and through the crevasses of an abyss, the quiet peaceful life which is mine no more, but which myriads of other men are leading still.

XXXVII.

THE Hôtel de Ville is a forbidding structure.

With its sharp, steep roof, its curious bell-tower, its great white clock-dial, its various floors with their little pillars, its thousand windows, its staircases worn smooth by countless footsteps, its two arches at the right and left, it stands there on a level with the Place de Grève, — a frowning, funereal edifice, with the marks of age all over its front, and so black that it looks black in the sunlight.

On days when an execution is to take place it vomits gendarmes from every door, and stares at the victim with all its windows.

And in the evening the dial which marks the hour is the only luminous spot on its gloomy façade.

XXXVIII.

It is quarter-past one.

This is the way I feel now : —

I have a violent pain in my head, my loins are cold, and my forehead is on fire. Every time that I rise or stoop it seems as if there was some liquid flowing inside my head, which washes my brain against the walls of my skull.

I have fits of convulsive trembling, and from time to time the pen falls from my hand as if I were struck by lightning.

My eyes smart as if they were filled with smoke.

I have a pain in my elbows.

Two hours and forty-five minutes more, and I shall be cured.

XXXIX.

THEY say that it is nothing, and that one does not suffer; that it is a painless end, and that death has been much simplified by this invention.

What about this six weeks of agony, and this death-rattle which lasts a whole day? What about the indescribable agony of this day, which passes so slowly and yet so quickly? What about this long ladder of tortures which leads up to the scaffold?

Apparently there is no suffering in all this.

Are not the convulsions the same whether the blood drains away, drop by drop, or the intelligence becomes extinct, thought by thought?

And then are they sure that there is no suffering? Who told them so? Did any one ever hear that a head that had been cut off stood up all bleeding on the edge of the basket, and cried to the people: "This is a fine invention. Stick to this. It can't be improved"?

Did Robespierre? Did Louis XVI.?

No, nothing of the sort! Less than a minute, less than a second, and the thing is done. Did they ever put themselves, even in thought, in the place of the man who lies there, just when the heavy blade falls and eats into the flesh, severs the nerves, and crushes the vertebræ? But what! a half-second! pain is done away with— Horror!

XL.

It is strange that I am forever thinking of the king. It makes no difference what I do, or how much I shake my head, there is a voice in my ear which constantly says : —

"There is in this very city, at this very moment, and not far away, in another palace, a man who also has guards at all his doors, a man who like you stands by himself among the people, — with the difference that he is as high as you are low. His whole life, minute by minute, is all glory, grandeur, pleasure. He is surrounded by affection, respect, veneration. The loudest voices speak low when they address him, and the haughtiest heads bow before him. Everything that he looks at is of silk and gold. At this moment he is holding a council of his ministers where every one is of his opinion ; or perhaps he is thinking about his hunting party to-morrow, or this evening's ball, sure that the fête will come off, and leaving to others the labor of preparing his amusements. But this man is made of flesh and blood, as you are ; and all that would be necessary to cause your ghastly scaffold to fall to pieces on the instant, and to restore to you life, liberty, fortune, everything, would be that he should write the seven letters of his name at the bottom of a bit of paper, or that his carriage should meet your tumbril in the street ! And he is kind, and perhaps would like nothing better ; and yet he will not interfere !"

XLI.

BUT enough of this ! let us show a bold front to death ; let us take the horrible thought in both hands, and look it squarely in the face. Let us ask it to describe what it is, find out what it wants of us, spell out the enigma, and look into the tomb before it is time.

It seems to me that as soon as my eyes are closed I shall see a great flood of light, and luminous oceans on which my soul will float forever. It seems to me that the sky will be alight with its own essence, that the stars will be dark blotches upon it, and that instead of being, as living men see them, golden specks upon black velvet, they will be black spots upon cloth of gold.

Or else, miserable wretch that I am, it will be a yawning, bottomless abyss, its walls hung with shadows, down which I shall fall and fall endlessly, surrounded by forms flitting about in the darkness.

Or else, when I awake after the blow, I shall find myself on some damp, level surface, crouching in the darkness, and turning over and over like a rolling head. It seems to me that there will be a mighty wind which will blow me along, and that I shall strike against other rolling heads here and there. At intervals there will be lakes and streams of an unfamiliar, lukewarm liquid ; everything will be black as night. When my eyes, as I roll along, are

turned upward, they will see naught but an opaque
sky, the dense strata of which will weigh upon them,
and make them heavy, and in the distance great
billows of smoke, blacker than the darkness. They
will also see little red sparks floating about, which,
as they come nearer, will become birds of flame.
And so it will be through all eternity.

It may be, too, that those who have died in the
Place de Grève assemble on dark winter nights
in the square which belongs to them. A pale and
ghastly crowd it must be, and I shall not fail
to join it. There will be no moon, and we shall
speak in whispers. The Hôtel de Ville will be
there, with its moth-eaten façade, its irregular roof,
and its clock-dial, which will, at some time, have
been pitiless to all of us. There will be a guillotine
from hell on the square, and on it a devil will exe-
cute an executioner; it will be at four o'clock in the
morning. We will take our turn at standing around
in a crowd.

It is probable that this is what will happen. But
if these dead men do return, in what shape do they
return? What part of their incomplete, mutilated
bodies do they retain? What do they choose? Is
the head or the body the ghost?

Alas! what does death do with the soul? in what
form does it leave it? What can death take from
or give to the soul? where does it place it? Does
it sometimes loan it eyes to look down upon the
earth and weep? Oh, for a priest! a priest who can
tell me that! I want a priest and a crucifix to kiss!

My God, always the same!

XLII.

I BEGGED them to let me sleep, and I threw myself upon my bed.

In truth, I had a rush of blood to my head, which made me sleep. It is my last sleep of this sort.

I had a dream.

I dreamed that it was dark. It seemed to me that I was in my office, with two or three of my friends. I don't know who they were.

My wife was in bed in the bedroom adjoining, and she and her child were asleep.

My friends and I were talking in undertones, and what we were saying terrified us.

Suddenly it seemed to me that I heard a faint noise somewhere in the other rooms of my suite, — a strange, indefinable noise.

My friends had also heard it. We listened; it was as if some one was turning a key very cautiously, or sawing through a bolt.

There was something about it that froze the blood in our veins; we were afraid. We thought that it must be robbers, at that late hour of the night.

We determined to investigate. I rose and took the candle. My friends followed me, in single file.

We passed through the bedroom. My wife and her child were asleep.

Then we reached the parlor.   There was nothing there.   The portraits looked down from their golden frames on the red hangings.   It seemed to me that the door between the parlor and dining-room was not in its usual place.

We went into the dining-room, and made the circuit of it.   I was walking ahead.   The door leading to the stairway was securely fastened, and so were the windows.   When I got to the stove, I noticed that the linen closet was open, and that the door was thrown back across the corner of the wall, as if to hide some one.

This surprised us.   We thought that there was some one behind the door.

I took hold of the door to close it; it resisted. I pulled harder, it yielded suddenly, and disclosed a little old woman, with hands hanging by her sides, and her eyes closed, standing without moving, as if she were nailed to the wall.

There was something ghastly about it, and my hair stands on end now to think of it.

" What are you doing there? " I asked the old woman.

No reply.

" Who are you? " I demanded.

Still no reply; she did not move nor open her eyes.

My friends said : —

" Doubtless she is the accomplice of those who broke in here for a criminal purpose ; they escaped when they heard us coming ; she had no time to fly, and so concealed herself there."

I questioned her again; she neither spoke nor moved nor looked at us.

One of us pushed her, and she fell to the floor.

She fell stiffly, like a piece of wood, or any lifeless thing.

We pushed her with our feet, and then two of us picked her up and put her against the wall again. She gave no sign of life. We shouted in her ear; she remained as dumb as if she were deaf.

At last we lost patience, and anger began to mingle with our fear. One of us said : —

" Put the candle under her chin."

I did as he suggested. Thereupon she half-opened one eye, — a vacant, dull, frightful eye, which could not be said to look.

I took the light away and said : —

" Ah! will you answer at last, old witch ? Who are you ? "

The eye closed again, as if of its own motion.

" This is too much," said the others. " Try the candle again ! She must be made to speak."

I put the light under the old woman's chin again.

Thereupon she slowly opened both eyes, looked at all of us, one after another, then stooped abruptly and blew out the candle with an icy breath. The next moment I felt three sharp teeth cut into my hand in the darkness.

I awoke trembling, and bathed in a cold perspiration.

The good chaplain was sitting at the foot of my bed, reading the prayer-book.

" Have I slept long ? " I asked.

"My son, you have slept an hour. They have brought your child. She is in yonder room, waiting to see you. I would n't allow you to be awakened."

"Oh!" I cried, "my daughter! bring me my daughter!"

XLIII.

She is fresh and rosy, she has great, black eyes, and is lovely.

She had on a little dress that is very becoming.

I took her in my arms, and put her on my knee, and kissed her hair.

Why not with her mother?

Her mother is ill, and her grandmother. Very well.

She looked at me wonderingly. Hugged and kissed and devoured with kisses, she made no remonstrance, but looked uneasily now and then at her nurse, who was weeping in a corner.

At last I was able to speak.

"Marie!" I said; "my little Marie!"

I strained her to my breast, swollen with sobs. She gave a little shriek.

"Oh! you hurt me, monsieur!"

Monsieur! It is a year since she saw me, poor child. She has forgotten me, face, voice, accent, all; and who could recognize me with this beard and these clothes and this deathly pallor? What! already blotted out of her memory, — the only one in which I cared to retain a place? What! I have already ceased to be a father! Am I doomed never to hear again that word, — that child's word, too

sweet to be retained in the language of grown men,
— *papa ?*

And yet I would have asked nothing more for the
forty years of life they are taking from me than
to hear it from that mouth just once, only once.

"Listen, Marie," I said, taking her two little
hands in mine, "don't you know me ?"

She gazed at me out of her lovely eyes, and
replied : —

"No, indeed ! "

"Look at me," I said.   "Really, don't you know
who I am ? "

"Yes.   A gentleman."

Alas ! to love ardently one single being in the
whole wide world, to love her with all one's love,
to have her before you, looking at you, speaking
to you, answering your questions, and to have her
not know who you are!   To long for consolation
from no one but her, and she the only human being
who does not know that you *must* have it because
you are about to die !

"Marie," I continued, "have you a papa ? "

"Yes, monsieur."

"Well, where is he ? "

She looked up at me with wide-open, wondering
eyes.

"Why, don't you know ? he is dead."

Then she cried out, for I almost let her fall.

"Dead ! " I said.   "Marie, do you know what
it is to be dead ? "

"Yes, monsieur.   He is in the ground and in the
sky."

She went on of her own accord : —

" I pray the good God for him every morning and evening at mamma's knees."

I kissed her on the forehead.

" Marie, say your prayer to me."

" I can't, monsieur. I must n't say my prayers in the daytime. Come to our house, this evening, and I will say it to you."

That was enough of that. I interrupted her.

" Marie, I am your papa."

" Oh ! " she said.

" Would you like me to be your papa ? " I added.

" No," she said, turning away her head, " my papa was much handsomer."

I covered her with kisses and with tears. She tried to jump out of my arms, crying : —

" You hurt me with your beard."

I put her back upon my knees, devouring her with my eyes, and questioned her.

" Marie, can you read ? "

" Yes, I can read nicely. Mamma makes me read my letters."

" Let us see ; read a little," I said, pointing to a paper which she had crumpled in one of her little hands.

She shook her pretty head.

" Oh ! I can only read fables."

" But just try. Come, read."

She unfolded the paper, and began to spell with her finger : —

" S, e, n, *sen*, t, e, n, c, e, *tence*, SENTENCE — "

I snatched it out of her hands. It was my

own death-sentence she was reading me ! Her nurse had bought the paper for a sou. It cost poor me much more than that.

There are no words to describe what I felt. My violence frightened her! she was almost weeping. Suddenly she said : —

"Give my paper back to me ; look! it's to play with."

I gave her to her nurse.

"Take her away," I said.

And I fell back upon my chair, disheartened, deserted, despairing. Now they may come ; I care for nothing now ; the last fibre of my heart is broken. I am ready for whatever they may do.

XLIV.

THE priest is kind-hearted, and the jailer. I think that they shed tears when I told the nurse to take my child away.

It is done. Now, I must stiffen my nerves, and think steadfastly of the executioner, the tumbril, the gendarmes, the crowd on the bridge, the crowd on the quay, the crowd at the windows, and of those who will come expressly on my account to the Place de Grève, which might be paved with the heads it has seen fall.

I believe I still have an hour to accustom myself to it all.

XLV.

ALL those will laugh and clap their hands and applaud. And among them, free to-day and unknown to the jailers, and hurrying joyously to the place of execution,— in that swarm of heads which will cover the square, there will be more than one that is doomed to follow mine sooner or later into the fatal basket. More than one who comes there on my account will come eventually on his own.

For these fated beings there is a fatal spot on the Place de Grève, a centre of attraction, a snare. They will hover around it until they are in it themselves.

XLVI.

MY dear little Marie! They have taken her back to her playthings; she gazes at the crowd through the window of the cab, and has forgotten all about the *gentleman*.

Perhaps I have time to write a few pages for her to read some day, so that fifteen years hence she may weep for this fatal day.

Yes, she must know my story from my own hand, and why the name I leave her is stained with blood.

XLVII.

MY HISTORY.

EDITOR'S NOTE. — We have been unable to find the leaves which should be inserted here. Perhaps, as those which follow would seem to imply, the condemned man had not time to write them. It was late when the thought occurred to him.

XLVIII.

FROM AN APARTMENT IN THE HÔTEL DE VILLE.

THE Hôtel de Ville! And so I am here at last. The horrible journey is done. The square is out yonder, and under my window the hateful mob, laughing and howling and waiting for me.

I tried in vain to stiffen my nerves and be brave, — my heart failed me. When I saw over the heads of the people those two long red arms with the black triangle at the end, standing between the lanterns of the quay, my heart failed me. I asked leave to make a dying declaration. They brought me here, and sent for some crown-attorney. I am now waiting for him; it is so much time gained.

Here he is.

The clock was striking three when they came to tell me it was time. I trembled like a leaf, as if I had been thinking of anything else for six hours, for six weeks, for six months. It came upon me at last like something unexpected.

They dragged me along their corridors and down their staircases. They pushed me through two wickets on the ground-floor into a narrow, dark, vaulted room, hardly lighted at all by this rainy, foggy day. There was a chair in the middle of the room. They told me to sit down, and I sat down.

Near the door and along the walls several persons were standing; beside the priest and the gendarmes there were three men.

The first, who was the tallest and oldest, was fat and red faced. He wore a redingote, and a shabby three-cornered hat. It was he.

It was the executioner, the servant of the guillotine. The others were his assistants.

I was no sooner seated than these last approached me from behind like cats; suddenly I felt cold steel amid my hair, and the shears grated against my ears.

My hair, cut at random, fell in bunches on my shoulders, and the man with the three-cornered hat gently brushed it away with his great hand.

The people in the room were talking in undertones.

There was a great noise outside, rising and falling on the air. I thought at first it was the river; but I soon knew from the roars of laughter that it was the crowd.

A young man, who was standing by the window writing with a pencil in a note-book, asked one of the turnkeys what it was they were doing.

"Making the prisoner's toilet," was the reply.

I understood that that will be in the newspaper to-morrow.

Suddenly one of the assistants took off my waist-coat, and the other seized my hands which were hanging at my side, and bound them behind my back. I felt the knot of a cord slowly tighten about my wrists. At the same time the first one was removing my cravat. My cambric shirt, the only relic that I still possessed of former days, made him hesitate a moment; then he began to cut away the collar.

At this ghastly precaution, at the chill touch of the knife on my neck, my elbows shook, and a stifled groan escaped me. The executioner's hand trembled.

"Excuse me, monsieur," he said. "Did I hurt you?"

These executioners are very kind men.

The crowd outside howled louder than ever.

A fat man with a pimply face offered me a hand-kerchief wet with vinegar to smell.

"Thanks," I said in the strongest voice I could command, " but I don't need it. I am all right."

Then one of the two stooped down and bound my feet loosely with a slender cord, so that I could take only very short steps. This cord they fastened to that with which my hands were tied.

Then the fat man threw my waistcoat over my shoulders and tied the sleeves together under my chin. With that everything was done that was to be done there.

Then the priest approached with his crucifix.

" Come, my son," he said.

The assistants put their hands under my armpits.
I stood up and walked. My steps were feeble, and
wavered as if I had two knees in each leg.

At that moment the outer door was thrown wide-
open. A tremendous uproar came in with the cold
air and the bright light, and reached me in the obscurity. Through the frowning doorway I suddenly
saw, amid the fast-falling rain, the myriad heads of
the yelling populace, crowded on the great steps of
the Palais de Justice; at the right, on a level with
the threshold, a row of mounted gendarmes, but I
could see only the forefeet and chests of their horses
through the low door ; in front, a detachment of soldiers in battle order; at the left, the rear end of a
tumbril with a ladder set up against it. An awful
picture, fittingly framed by a prison door.

For that dreaded moment I had reserved all my
courage. I took three steps forward, and appeared
in the doorway.

" There he is! there he is!" cried the crowd.
" He is coming out at last ! "

Those who were nearest clapped their hands.
Well as they love their king, his appearance would
gratify them much less.

It was a common cart, with an emaciated horse,
and a driver in a blue smock frock with red figures
on it, like those worn by the market-gardeners around
Bicêtre.   The fat man in the three-cornered hat went
up first.

" Good day, Monsieur Sanson ! " cried the children
hanging to the bars.

An assistant came next.

" Bravo, Mardi ! " the children cried again.

They both sat down on the forward seat.

It was my turn. I ascended the ladder with a reasonably firm step.

" He walks well ! " said a woman standing by the gendarmes.

This horrible praise gave me courage. The priest took his seat beside me. They had placed me on the rear seat, with my back to the horse. I shuddered at this last attention. There was a humane idea at the bottom of it.

I tried to look around me. Gendarmes in front, gendarmes behind ; and everywhere the crowd, the crowd, the crowd ; the square was a sea of heads.

A squad of mounted gendarmes awaited me at the outer gate of the palace.

The officer gave the word. The cart and its escort started as if they were blown forward by a shout from the populace.

We passed through the gate. As the cart turned toward the Pont au Change, the square sent up a mighty roar from pavement to house-tops, and the bridges and quays replied so vigorously that the ground shook.

At that point the squad that was awaiting us joined the escort.

" Hats off ! hats off ! " shouted a thousand voices together, as if for the king.

Then I laughed a ghastly laugh, and said to the priest : —

" Their hats, and my head."

We went at a foot pace.

The Quai aux Fleurs was one mass of sweet perfume; it is the flower-market day. The flower-girls left their bouquets to look at me.

Opposite the quay, just before you come to the square tower which forms the corner of the palace, there are cabarets, and their *entresols* were filled with spectators, delighted with their fine places, especially the women. It must be a good day for the proprietors.

Tables, chairs, scaffoldings, and carts, everything is let. Everything is groaning with spectators. Dealers in human blood are crying at the top of their voices: —

"Who wants to buy a place?"

I became furiously angry with the savages. I longed to shout: —

"Who wants to buy my place?"

Meanwhile the tumbril rumbled along. At every step the crowd melted away behind it, and I could see them with my wandering eyes hurrying to find standing-room at other points along my route.

As we rode into the Pont au Change I happened to glance back and to my right. My eyes rested on an isolated black tower on the other quay, towering above the houses and bristling with sculpture. At its summit, I could see two stone monsters seated, with their profile turned toward me. I have no idea why I asked the priest what tower it was.

"Saint-Jacques-la-Boucherie," the executioner replied.

I cannot say how it happened, but through the mist, and in spite of the fine, white rain which streaked the air like a network of spider's webs, nothing of what took place around me escaped my notice. Each detail caused its own torture. Words are powerless to describe my emotions.

Toward the centre of the Pont-au-Change, which was so crowded that we went forward with great difficulty, the horror of my position took strong hold of me. I feared that I should faint, — my last touch of vanity! Then I resolutely determined to be blind and deaf to everything except the priest, whose words, continually interrupted by the uproar, I could hardly hear.

I took the crucifix and kissed it.

" Have pity on me, O my God !" I said. And I tried to lose myself in that thought.

But every jolt of the cart shook me terribly, and I suddenly felt intensely cold. The rain had soaked through my clothes, and had wet my scalp through my closely-cropped hair.

" Are you trembling with cold, my son ? " the priest inquired.

" Yes," I replied.

Alas ! not with cold alone.

At the end of the bridge some women pitied me because I was so young.

We reached the fatal quay. I began to lose all sense of sight and hearing. All those voices, and the heads at the windows and doors of houses and shops, and hanging to the lantern brackets ; the craving, cruel spectators ; the vast crowd, in which every one

knew me, and I knew not a soul; the paved road-
way, lined with human faces— I was drunk, stupid,
mad. The weight of so many looks fastened upon
you is an intolerable thing.

So I reeled on my seat, paying no further attention
even to the priest and the crucifix.

In the tumult which surrounded me I could no
longer distinguish the exclamations of compassion
from the shouts of joy, the laughter from the sorrow,
the voices from the other noises; it all made a confused roaring in my brain, as if it were a copper
vessel.

My eyes mechanically read the signs over the shop
doors.

Once I felt a strange desire to turn my head and
see what I was going toward. It was a last attempt
at bravado on the part of the mind. But the body
would not respond; my neck was paralyzed, and
had died in anticipation.

I saw, at my left, beyond the river, only one tower
of Notre-Dame, which, when seen from that point,
hides the other. It is the one where the flag is.
There were many people there, who ought to have a
good view.

And the cart went on and on, and the shops passed,
and one sign was followed by another, written, painted,
gilded, and the people laughed and trampled along in
the mud, and I let myself go with the current, as
men do in their dreams.

Suddenly the succession of shops which kept my
eyes busy was broken by the corner of a square; the
voice of the crowd became louder and shriller and

more joyous than ever; the cart suddenly stopped, and I nearly fell face downward on the boards.   The priest held me up.   "Courage!" he whispered. Then they brought a ladder to the rear of the cart; he gave me his arm, I climbed down, took one step, and turned to take another, but could not.   Between the two lanterns of the quay I had seen a sinister object.

Oh! it was the grim reality at last!

I stopped, as if already staggering from the fatal blow.

"I have a dying declaration to make!" I cried, weakly.

They brought me here.

I asked leave to write my last wishes.   They unbound my hands, but the cord is here, all ready, and the other is still around my ankles.

XLIX.

A JUDGE, a commissioner or a magistrate of some sort, has arrived. I implored him to pardon me, clasping my hands, and dragging myself along on my knees. He replied by asking me, with a deadly smile, if that was all I had to say to him.

"Pardon! pardon!" I repeated, "or five minutes' respite, in pity's name!

"Who knows? perhaps it will come. It is so awful, at my age, to die such a death! Pardons have often arrived at the last moment. And who should be pardoned, monsieur, if not I?"

That infernal executioner! he approached the judge to tell him that the execution is fixed for a certain hour, that that hour is approaching, that he is responsible, and furthermore that it rains and there is danger of the thing becoming rusty.

"Oh! for pity's sake! one minute to wait for my pardon! or I will defend myself, — I will bite!"

The judge and the executioner have gone out. I am alone, — alone with two gendarmes.

Oh! the horrible people, with their hyena cries! Who knows that I may not escape, that I may not be rescued if my pardon— It is impossible that they will not pardon me!

Ah! the villains! I think I hear them coming up the stairs.

FOUR O'CLOCK.

NOTES.

1829.

WE give here for the benefit of persons interested in this variety of literature, the ballad in *argot*, with the explanation thereof, taken from a copy which we found among the papers of the condemned man; orthography and chirography are both faithfully reproduced in this fac-simile. The meaning of the slang terms was in the condemned man's handwriting; there are also two lines inserted in the last stanza which seem to have been written by him; the balance is in another hand. It is probable that he was struck with the song, but remembered it imperfectly, and so tried to procure it, and that this copy was furnished him by some penman in the jail.

The only thing which the fac-simile does not reproduce is the condition of the paper on which the original was written; it is yellow, soiled, and broken at the creases.

1881.

THE original manuscript of the " Last Day of a Condemned," has on the margin of the first page: "Tuesday, October 14, 1828." At the foot of the last page: " Night of December 25–26, 1828, 3 o'clock in the morning."

THE END.

CPSIA information can be obtained
at www.ICGtesting.com
Printed in the USA
BVHW070145250520
580231BV00003B/462